THE RUSSIAN POPE

David Chappell

Copyright © 2024 David Chappell

All rights reserved.

The right of David Chappell to be identified as author of this work has been asserted by him in accordance with sections 77 and 78 of the Copyright, Designs and Patent Act 1988.

Some of the persons and institutions do or did exist but none of the opinions or actions attributed to them have any basis in fact. Other characters are totally fictitious and are not intended to represent any real persons living or dead.

NOVELS BY THE SAME AUTHOR

The Coat of Arms

CONTENTS

PROLOGUE
1 LINANKA
2 SPARTOV
3 ARTHUR
4 ARRIVALS
5 DEATHS
6 MAURICE MAKES A FRIEND
7 CONCLAVE
8 SPARTOV
9 SUBSTITUTION
10 VATICAN
11 ARTHUR GETS READY
12 GOODBYE KUTZNOV
13 PROBLEMS
14 LIA HAS FUN
15 MORE PROBLEMS
16 ARTHUR'S SAFE HOUSE
17 MOSCOW IS IMPATIENT
18 SEEDS
19 SOUTH AMERICA
20 GRIMALDI AND OTHERS
21 VISITS
22 DEATH AND KIDNAP
23 AT THE SAFE HOUSE
24 FATHER ARETZI
25 PAY DAY
26 AFTERMATH
EPILOGUE
ACKNOWLEDGEMENTS

PROLOGUE

1956

Snow fell in great clods of white. It fell throughout the State of Wisconsin and shrouded the banks of the upper reaches of the Mississippi river. Smaller particles separated from the rest were taken up by the wind and swirled around in eddies, finally coming to rest to form strange and transitory sculptures around the edge of the pitch pine forests. Town folk kept to their homes, cabins and apartments or died of exposure in the lee of brick walls in dark places. Abandoned cars formed mounds at first in the white blanket and then disappeared. Life came to a standstill for a week until the snow stopped falling.

The snow ploughs made brave efforts to clear a path down the centre of the main roads for essential services.

When Spring came and the snow retreated, the town mortuaries were filled with the deep-frozen casualties. Young Bobby McGrath, who had left home in the middle of the big fall, had got no further than the crossroads on the inter-State highway. Seth Greenhough never got back from his illicit liaison with Karen Greatorex. Vagrants, hippies, farmers and unwary travellers from the big cities to the south were among the dead. Some had also taken the opportunity to settle old debts and there were corpses with bullet holes and knife wounds. It was traditionally the busy season for homicide.

Of all the bodies which strewed the desks of the various chiefs of homicide, one was singular. All clothing had been removed, as had the hands and feet. The teeth had been drawn and the face smashed to a pulp.

Lieutenant Oscar Wennant, who was put in charge of the case, figured that the corpse could not be that of an ordinary vagrant. It must be someone who could be easily recognised, hence the steps taken to ensure identification would be difficult. It was still mighty unusual, although not unknown, for a murderer to go to such lengths.

The lieutenant asked the pathology lab for every significant detail about the body, DNA identification being then unknown, and circulated them to every State police department and, as an added precaution, to the Canadian police as well. If DNA had been in use, the body would not have been found. Indeed, it is likely the owner of the body would not have been dead.

But the owner clearly was dead. The details were scant. The body was male, about five feet ten (with assumed feet), light brown hair, grey eyes (probably). No distinguishing marks of any kind were found. The age was estimated to be about thirty.

During the six months which followed Wennant found himself with over three hundred possible contenders for the name of 'corpse of the year', as he called it. At the end of the six months, he had whittled the list down to three: a petty gangster who had fled his gaming debts in Las Vegas, a young man who had suddenly vanished from his nuptial bed in Nevada and a prominent young lawyer missing from his house in Ontario since last Christmas.

The spot where the body was found provided no clues. It had been turned up by the snow plough on a road, miles from the nearest town. It had most likely been dumped from a car just before the big fall of snow. It was quite impossible to check what vehicles had travelled along the road.

The lieutenant finally put away the file, together with photographs of the three missing men. If positive identification of any of them turned up he could cross them off until, hopefully, he was left with only one. Then, at least, he could give the corpse a name, or so he thought. He was not to know that the corpse was none of the missing men.

Earlier that same year, Ralph Walsh returned to his post in Washington DC after a long convalescence. The virus had struck quite suddenly and, being unmarried and without any close relatives, he had undergone treatment in hospital and then taken two months off at a private nursing home in the country to complete his recovery.

It was understandable that he did not seem to be quite himself when he got back to work. He was paler, naturally, and he was not quite so outgoing as previously. It was to be expected also that he should be a little slow slotting into the routine. Everyone helped him to readjust and soon he had resumed his climb up the ladder of promotion nearer the centre of government. He was very bright and full of potential.

1960

When Edgar Brown set off for his winter holiday in Switzerland on the 22nd November, he went with the good wishes of his superior in the Ministry of Defence in London. Edgar was a conscientious worker and destined to rise rapidly through the ranks of the Civil Service. Although only thirty-one, he was already a principal assistant in the department. Edgar's father had been an Anglican Vicar before his death the year before, leaving Edgar alone. From his father he had inherited a certain reservation of character which was not considered to be a disadvantage in his chosen career.

Despite his reserve, Edgar was generally well liked and it was something of a shock, therefore, when his friends at the Ministry heard that he had sustained a fractured leg and collar bone while climbing.

Edgar did not return in fact until after Christmas. He was rather pale but, on the whole, a little less withdrawn than usual which was generally considered to be a good thing. After all, travel was supposed to broaden the mind. Everyone, even his superior, agreed that he had changed for the better.

1966

The workman who spotted a body floating in the Rhine telephoned the police immediately. The police launch that recovered it was staffed by hardened veterans who were used to unpleasant sights. Even so, one of them was physically sick when they got the corpse on deck. It must have been in the water for weeks and it was badly decomposed. It was not that which induced nausea, however, but the fact that the hands and feet had been removed and the front of the skull battered and broken. It was clear, too, that all the teeth had been taken out.

No identification being possible, the body was listed as murdered and quietly buried.

By 1972, nineteen bodies had been mutilated in the same bizarre fashion; although only two were ever found.

1. LINANKA

1972

Moscow has an unusual layout. The Kremlin, seat of all power, forms the central core on the northern bank of the river. Around it run concentric lines of boulevards gathered together by a roughly circular ring road marking the city boundary. The length of this road is one hundred and five kilometres.

There are a few really old buildings in Moscow but, particularly since the Second World War, a great many rather severe modern structures in glass and concrete housing people in flats and apartments, exhibitions and collections in galleries and museums, functions of government in a variety of buildings ranging from the large, bold and pompous to the small, self-effacing and secretive.

The vast Linanka complex was situated several kilometres outside the outer ring road, to the north of the city. It was set down without deference to its surroundings, four-square among the trees of a small forest. The complex covered an area of about 5.7 hectares. The walls, built of stone were 7.6 metres high and massive. Somewhat taller square towers were built at the corners and at intervals along the walls. From these structures, searchlights illuminated the cleared area around the complex and machine-gunners shot without question any moving thing within that area. There was only one entrance.

A bright two-storey building stood in the very centre of the complex, housing the living and working accommodation of the inhabitants. The guards were housed within the four corner structures.

Between the two-storey building and the surrounding walls the area resembled nothing so much as a film set, but a set in which many different films were being shot at the same time. In one section a fair reproduction of part of London's Piccadilly Circus was fabricated. Selected portions of many of the world's capital cities covered most of the available space. Here and there, pleasant garden areas were laid out in various styles: English, Japanese, Italian. Fountains played and small London taxis rubbed fenders with preposterous American cars. Typical dwellings, fully furnished in the style of various countries lined the inner face of the external walls. Regular amendments to the layout were carried out by a permanent gang of tradesmen.

The idea had germinated in the mind of Laurentiy Beria during the final years of Stalin's life. It was shortly afterwards that the extraordinary complex had been devised by an unknown Russian architect, then erected with the unwilling help of hundreds of prisoners of war and refugees from the central stage of the European conflict. All who laboured on the final stages of the complex had disappeared.

Extraordinary secrecy surrounded the establishment and all who worked there were closely watched by KGB agents. The guards knew little of the purpose of the complex and if they showed any curiosity, it was dealt with by summary execution. The policy of kill first and ask no questions at all was remarkably effective, if not reassuring to the staff. Total security was maintained. The guards did alternate three monthly spells of duty. Holidays were strictly controlled under watchful eyes. Whole families were liquidated at the slightest hint of indiscretion.

The staff, numbering about seventy-five, who inhabited the central two-story building were subject to even more careful security checks.

There were three separate departments: Physical Attributes and Co-relation, headed by Dr Fritz Klein with four assistants; Languages with forty staff and Behavioural Techniques with thirty staff. The names of the departments are roughly translated from the Russian. Dr Klein was a tall thin man with parchment white skin and wire rimmed tinted spectacles concealing watery grey eyes. He was born in Germany in 1912 and owed his position to his skill in an unusual form of surgery in which he reached perfection in Belsen concentration camp until the final stages of World War Two. He was astute enough to leave the camp early when the end was in sight, and make his way, not to the British and American armies but, to the advancing Russian troops. He narrowly escaped death but survived by the simple expedient of convincing the Russians that his experience could prove valuable. He was generally considered to be borderline mentally unstable but it could not be denied that he did his work carefully, accurately and with tremendous dedication.

From 1970, the officer in charge of this highly specialised establishment was Colonel Nikolai Kutznov.

Kutsnov was a huge figure, well over six feet tall with close cut grey hair and weighing in at something over one hundred and forty kilograms. At the time of his appointment he was about fifty years old. His face was curiously featureless as though it had been moulded out of plasticine and then smacked against an unyielding wall. In profile, a straight line could be drawn from forehead to chin through which his nose would have projected hardly at all. Although not without humour, he smiled rarely. Indeed, his face showed little emotion of any kind. Long years in the KGB had taught him to keep his secret impulses well under control. He remained motionless unless some action was positively required. He spoke only when it was absolutely necessary and exercised the utmost economy in both. In this way he preserved the maximum time for thinking. Careful thought was essential in his work. His carefully organised community was devoted to the production of a very singular kind of agent.

The concept was simple, but the creation of the agent was complex and time-consuming. First, Colonel Nikolai Kutznov, in conjunction with a very special KGB committee in Moscow would prepare a list of people working at the heart of government and other departments in countries of the Western Alliance. The people on the list would be bright and assertive but not usually in the higher ranks of their chosen professions. Special investigators, usually based in the Soviet embassy to the country of the person being targeted, would compile a detailed file of everything concerning the target. This was sent to the Linanka complex.

An agent, bearing a passing resemblance to the target would be chosen, trained and operated on until he or she was indistinguishable from the target. At an appropriate time, the agent would be substituted for the target, often before the target returned to work after a long holiday or fake stay in a remote hospital so that colleagues would not easily be able to compare the agent with recent memories of the target. The target would be secretly killed and the body relieved of its hands, feet and teeth and the face completely destroyed to make identification impossible. Ideally what remained of the body would be cremated or dropped into the ocean far from land.

If either action was impossible, it was disposed of in some other secure way. There were only two instances of target bodies being disposed of in some other way: one in the USA and the other in Germany. Although the bodies were found and reported to the local police, they were never identified. Nevertheless, the operatives responsible for the bungled disposal of the bodies were themselves disposed of on Kutznov's orders.

In May 1972 Colonel Kutznov sat at his desk, his vast bulk overflowing the chair so that it creaked in protest whenever he adjusted his position. In front of him on the green baize of the desk top was a solitary sheet of paper containing a list of the agents. Kutznov had been studying the names for over two hours. He knew all there was to know about the background of each of them. He leaned forward and pressed a button near his right hand. The door opened immediately and a young man in military uniform entered. He was Kutznov's principal assistant. He was used to these meeting and to his master's apparent inertia.

'Recommendations?' Kutznov was as impassive as ever, his eyes two tiny currants in a sea of blancmange.

The young man stood at attention opposite the desk. He flipped back the plastic cover on the clipboard he held. 'The three most recent agents are progressing well. Dr Klein has finished his initial work on them. At the present rate of progress, they should be ready in two years. The next five agents are almost ready and could be placed next year, in theory.' He knew the policy regarding the placing of agents as well as Kutsnov himself. 'The remaining agents are ready now and it might be a good idea to place one of them, the French one, as soon as possible. The German agent is redundant, because the target has suddenly died. Shall I take the necessary steps?'

'Yes.' Kutznov picked up a stubby black pencil and drew a black line through one of the fifteen entries on the paper in front of him. 'Proceed with the French substitution,' he said.

The young man snapped the plastic cover over his clipboard and clicked his heels. He was about to leave when he paused as a thought struck him. He turned back to Kutznov who was still looking at his sheet of paper, pencil in hand. 'Have you come to any decision regarding Andrei Spartov?'

'Not yet.' Kutznov did not bother to look up. The young man nodded and left.

2. SPARTOV

Thursday 13 April 1972

Andrei Spartov was churning with envy when he heard that two of his fellow agents were shortly to be placed elsewhere. His envy would have been tempered if he had known that one of them would be placed in a hole in the ground just outside the complex.

In his clinical room Kutznov had dismissed the redundant agent from his mind. He pondered the question of Andrei Spartov. The time was ripe but he had received no reply to the query which he had put to the KGB general who reserved such sensitive matters to himself. Kutznov knew that it was important not to overdo the placing of these special agents. The more there were, the greater the chance that the elaborate plot would be uncovered. Although that might not be absolutely fatal to the continuance of the scheme as a whole, it would necessarily put the Western Allies on their guard and make future activities more difficult. At present they placed no more than one or two in a year. The Spartov placing was a little more ambitious than usual and it would have to be handled with great care.

It is perfectly true that events are largely shaped by the circumstances of the moment. The successful refer to it as being in the right place at the right time; the world's failures talk of being in the wrong place at the wrong time. Although it is necessary to fulfil both criteria, as to place and time to be a success; a failure is merely required to satisfy one of them. It no doubt explains why there are more of the latter than the former.

To some extent, of course, such descriptions are subjective, relating only to the speaker. One man's failure is another's triumph. The first men to conquer Everest were only first because all others before them failed. During a war, one country's victory is another's defeat. How far chance plays its part is a matter for speculation.

Andrei Spartov owed his place at the KGB establishment for special agents (whether that was in itself success or failure depends upon the point of view) to a number of factors, none of which were under his control and, therefore, qualify for the description of 'chance'.

He was born in 1928 of relatively prosperous parents. His father, whom he remembered as a quiet worried man, had a minor government job in the city of Kiev; which, nevertheless, carried certain privileges with it. His mother was warm and full of common sense. She had been born in Czechoslovakia and went to Russia as a young girl to work on a farm. She had met his father and it had been a traditional courtship culminating in their marriage and the subsequent birth of Andrei. Two years later a daughter, Petrova, was born but she had died in infancy and there had been no more children.

The family kept themselves apart from their neighbours or perhaps the reverse was true, on account of Mr Spartov's job. When Andrei was nine, he and his mother went to visit his grandmother, his mother's mother, in Czechoslovakia. She lived in Prague and it was arranged that they should live there for about six months. During that period young Andrei became reasonably fluent in that language.

They returned to Kiev and Mr Spartov senior had resumed the normal uneventful life of the family of a government employee. Excitement was missing until the Germans invaded, then there was an abundance of it. The family survived the war but the appalling hardships left Andrei's father broken in health and spirit, his mother harder and less approachable. The Fascist invasion left a deep scar on Andrei's soul. After his compulsory period of military service in the Army, he decided to stay and make his career, as he thought, in the army. Being quick-witted and intelligent, he made good progress and, by the time he was thirty-seven, he was a full major. His duties carried him to various parts of the Soviet Union. Unlike some of his fellow officers, who were rough hard drinking professionals, he was sensitive and took his pleasure in books. Everything he read convinced him, not that conviction was lacking, of the necessity to further the communist ideology. The poverty he encountered could be blamed upon the machinations of the purveyors of capitalism and its manifestation in western countries. Andrei Spartov was a totally committed, unquestioning communist.

The right place for Andrei Spartov was the army barracks on the outskirts of Leningrad one Spring day in 1972.

'Colonel Rostock has arrived.'

'Ask him to come in.' Major Spartov rose from his desk. He looked somewhat older than his forty-four years but he was still a fine figure, rather under six feet tall with broad shoulders and tanned face of the habitual athlete. The drab grey of his uniform heightened, rather than otherwise, his commanding presence. His hair was receding and cut short, lightly tinged with grey. His face was rugged and powerful rather than handsome, with piercing blue eyes. He was feeling nervous as he waited for Colonel Rostock to enter. He knew very well that the colonel was a member of the uniformed branch of the KGB and visits from the KGB usually boded no good and were to be avoided. He had not been informed of the purpose of the visit and he looked around the office apprehensively. His eyes took in the pale green walls covered with maps and charts, the bookcase filled with books on strategy, tactics and socialist philosophy, the table covered with a contour model showing the next day's manoeuvres and, finally the desk behind which he stood. It was old and worn just as he felt at that moment.

The door opened and Colonel Rostock entered. Unexpectedly, he was not in uniform. He wore a double-breasted dark blue suit which hung untidily on his chunky body. He was a startling contrast to Spartov. Middle-aged, dark haired and pudgy-faced, his eyes were set just too closely together for comfort. They clasped damp hands and, without further ceremony, Rostock sat down. Spartov followed suit.

'I will come straight to the point Major. Are you happy with your present life?'

Spartov answered carefully. 'Certainly Colonel. I am furthering the cause of our country in some small way.'

'Good, that is just it; in some small way. However, would you be prepared to carry out a dangerous mission which would be of inestimable value to the ideals we all share?'

'I am prepared, at a moment's notice, to move wherever I can be of most use.'

'I won't mince words with you. In a cabinet in my office I have thousands of files of all serving officers in the Army. I have a very special job. I match faces and general physical characteristics.' Spartov's puzzlement showed in his face.

'I can only tell you a little more at this stage,' Rostock obviously relished the power his organisation conferred on him. 'When I find that certain physical characteristics match, I pay a visit like this one, to interview the candidate in person.' He unzipped his briefcase and took out some photographs which he compared with the seated figure of Andei Spartov. He held the photographs in just such a way that Spartov could not see them. At length he seemed satisfied and tucked them away again.

'I note that your parents and your sister are dead and that you are not married although you are not unacquainted with the opposite sex. You indulge yourself in that direction moderately and you drink rarely. Your medical record is satisfactory for our purposes and you will shortly be summoned to Moscow. To be precise to the Linanka Complex. A replacement will be arranged for you.' Colonel Rostock rose abruptly and with a smile, whether of pleasure or malice Spartov could not decide, he left the office. Spartov, who had risen to his feet, slumped down in his chair, not certain whether he had been removed in disgrace or promoted to higher office. He had heard rumours about Linanka, everyone had. It was said to be a high security prison from which no one, not even the guards, returned. Was he to be moved to take charge of that place? Was that why Rostock had made sure that he had no relatives who would miss him? Surely not, he had always understood that the KGB were in charge of the

Linanka. He was not a member of the KGB, but Rostock was.

Exactly one week later, he had stood in front of Major Kutznov in Linanka. During the previous forty-eight hours, since his arrival in the complex, he had had a thorough medical examination from Dr Klein. Measurements of every part of his body had been taken; he had been X-rayed, scanned, pinched, pricked and subjected to every standard physical check together with a few more which the elderly doctor had concocted apparently for his own amusement. Just at the point he felt he had emerged from a particularly vicious mincing machine, he was taken to a bare-walled room and interrogated for a couple of hours about every conceivable topic. He swayed a little as he faced the massive figure of the Commandant.

'Sit down.'

Spartov gratefully relaxed and sat down in the slightly too wide, slightly too hard and, in short, thoroughly uncomfortable chair facing the desk. Kutznov had a file open in front of him. He sighed audibly not, as Spartov supposed, because he had bad news to impart but because he had no alternative except to embark upon a bout of talking.

'Major Spartov, your rank is now removed and you are reduced to the status of an ordinary Soviet citizen. This step is taken, not because you have committed any offence, it is not a disgrace, quite the contrary. You have been selected to join an elite group of men who will render great services to our country. You will not leave this complex for perhaps six or seven years and when you leave you will never, ever, return to Russia. Your task will be of great importance, can you face the prospect?'

'If it will advance the cause of world communism, I will willingly give my life.' It was no more than Kutznov expected. He was used to dealing with well-read intelligent young fanatics and he found them easier to manage than the run of the mill KGB thug.

'In that case, I will give you brief details. You have been chosen because you bear a remarkable similarity to a moderately highly placed gentleman. You will be trained in everything you need to know and you will be expected to absorb all the information we can give you about this man. We want you to become this man in appearance, gesture, words and actions. In every way except thought. When we consider the time is appropriate, we will arrange a substitution and you will be expected to carry on your life under your new identity, imparting such information as might be useful to us, via a contact whom we will arrange in due course. You will never be able to escape from your new identity except, of course, by your eventual death. Even then, you will be buried under your new name. The mission is onerous but rewarding.' Kutznov sagged. It really was quite exhausting.

Spartov found that he was leaning forward gripping the arms of the chair. Never to see Russia again; but against that the opportunity to contribute something positive. Could he really absorb the personality of another so easily and would he ever feel free again? Probably not, he would be forever on his guard against a slip of the tongue. Now he knew what was meant by the rumour that no one ever escaped from Linanka. As if reading his mind, Kutznov interrupted his chain of thought.

'Your victim, as we refer to them, is at first sight, a strange one: Wenceslas Tadeo Celavsky, Bishop of Brno, in southern Moravia, Czechoslovakia. He is somewhat older than you, forty-nine, but he looks rather younger than his years, as you look older. Celavsky is important because he is an extremely clever man, intelligent, learned and highly esteemed in his Church. We think that, before too long, he will be transferred to work in the Vatican, probably in the office of the Secretary of State. He was previously papal nuncio to Chile and later the Philippines before being appointed to his present position last year. A nuncio is the head of the Vatican's Diplomatic Mission in a particular state. It is something like but not the same as an embassy. Needless to say, we are extremely interested in the secrets which pass through the office of the Secretariat of State and we are looking for another agent to ensure that we learn all the secrets. The Vatican has, by virtue of its status as headquarters of the Roman Catholic Church, tentacles of influence in every country.'

Kutznov pressed his buzzer. The young man from the next office came in and Kutznov, visibly glad that the interview was over, nodded. The young man shepherded Spartov out into the long corridor which ran the full length of the upper storey.

Spartov had had no opportunity to examine his new home. He felt tired, his head ached and the corridor seemed endless. The young man, whose name was Joseph, opened one of the many doors.

'Remember the number. This is your room now for the remainder of your stay. Do not be surprised at anything you see. Get a good night's rest and you will be awakened tomorrow by a personal bell. Each agent is woken at a different time to correspond with the personal waking hours of his victim. Unfortunately for you, Bishop Celavsky gets up every morning at six-thirty.' With a laugh which was not unfriendly, he bade Spartov goodnight and walked off down the corridor again.

Spartov switched on the light and stood absolutely still for a moment, startled by what he saw. He closed the door and examined the room which was to be his home. It was roughly five metres square. A simple iron bedstead stood against one wall on which hung a large wooden crucifix. On a bedside cabinet stood a faded photograph of a man and a woman and, behind it, a shiny chrome alarm clock and a reading lamp. Against the wall opposite the window was a prie-dieu and another crucifix. Over by the window stood an old-fashioned roll-topped desk surmounted by a glass-fronted bookcase. Closer inspection revealed that the books were volumes of Church history, theology, directories and a many-volume encyclopaedia. There were one or two books on mountain climbing and other sports. A straight-backed chair completed the furniture. The floor had no carpet but a rug was laid near the bed. The walls were papered in a pale flowery pattern. Heavy blue velvet curtains hung at the window.

A door to the left of the bed opened onto a small bathroom but the door opposite yielded the biggest surprise – a tiny chapel, completely fitted out with altar, vestments and two prie-dieux. In contrast to the bedroom, it was well, almost luxuriously, appointed.

Spartov undressed and climbed laboriously into bed. He noticed a packet of cigarettes and a box of matches behind the clock. He did not smoke, but obviously Bishop Celavsky did. Spartov had already correctly surmised that the room was an exact replica of the one used by Celavsky in the episcopal residence at Brno.

He lay on his back in the darkness. Obviously, the whole project was highly organised. He wondered how long it would take him to get under the skin of this foreign prelate who represented everything that Spartov despised. Could he really carry out the sham of worshipping a non-existent God? He was curious about his victim. How corrupt would he be? It was well known in Russia that, of all the corrupt institutions of the West, the Roman Catholic Church was the worst. He remembered that some of the people in Kiev went to church. He was not sure, but he assumed that it was a Russian variation of the Catholic church, he had never thought about it before. All superstitious nonsense of course.

He drifted into a dream about a large fat man dressed in rich robes studded with gems of every description. He had a golden chalice in one hand and a naked girl lay across his knee. He took deep drafts from the cup, spilling its contents down his robes and onto the girl. The chalice turned into a huge dagger with which he repeatedly slashed at the girl who squirmed and squealed with delight. The image faded and returned many times until he recognised himself drinking and slashing. He sat up abruptly in a sweat of fear. It was some time before sleep returned.

Friday 5th May 1972

A loud shrill bell awoke him. His bedroom door opened and an indistinct face told him that he had half an hour to get washed, dressed and present himself at room 40 on the floor below. His clothes had been removed during the night and a set of clerical garments in black with red buttons had replaced them.

After washing, he had some difficulty in donning the clerical garb and the sash. Exactly how he was to wear the gold crucifix and chain also puzzled him but he hung it around his neck and hoped for the best. It seemed a trifle long and he tucked it into his sash as he went out of the door and scanned the corridor for some clue to his destination.

It had been dark when he had ascended the staircase after his interrogation and the corridor took on a more cheerful aspect in the daylight which flooded down through domed rooflights set at intervals.

He remembered that, to enter his room, he had turned into a door on his left as he proceeded down the corridor. Therefore, if he now turned left upon leaving his room, he should continue down the corridor rather than retrace his steps. He decided to do that as he was near the end of the corridor anyway. Through double doors he found the staircase and, when he arrived at the bottom, room 40 faced him across the corridor.

When he entered the room, he saw that it was a dining room, pleasantly if not extravagantly furnished with a table and sixteen chairs, dark carpet and large windows which looked out over a small garden with a fountain playing in the middle. The glass had a subtle bronze tinge and he was to learn later that, from the outside, it was impossible to see into the building.

A small fat man with close cropped hair and a cheerful smile got up from the table and addressed him. It took Spartov a few minutes to realise that the man was speaking Czech. Spartov was grateful to his mother at that moment for encouraging him to remain proficient in the language of her people. The man, who appeared to be about the same age as Spartov, repeated himself.

'Good morning, My Lord.' Spartov stared and the fat man's face broke into a broad grin. 'We don't often have the pleasure of entertaining such high ranking, or indeed any, Roman Catholic prelates in this humble establishment.' The fat man was obviously enjoying Spartov's discomfiture. 'I shouldn't tease you, but you will have to get used to your part. I'm afraid that you will play it from this moment for the rest of your life. Let me introduce myself. My name is Granky. I will be your personal tutor during your stay. You will be spoken to only in Czech and every day you will attend lessons so that you become totally fluent. I am speaking slowly at present but, as time goes on you will find that you will begin the think in Czech. Bishop Celavsky speaks only a little Russian, but he is fluent in Spanish and Italian and he can manage to conduct a conversation in English and French. Of course, he also knows Latin. It will be necessary for you to attain his level of proficiency in all these languages. But let us eat and we will discuss your particular project over breakfast.'

Granky busied himself at a small hatch Spartov had not noticed before, while Spartov seated himself at the table and wondered whether he had been a little unwise to agree to take part in this scheme. Granky, meanwhile, brought a tray filled with the paraphernalia of breakfast to the table. He moved with curiously fussy little actions, patting the tablecloth, adjusting and readjusting knives and forks.

'You will find it easier than you think. The teaching and learning will be intensive and the languages are the least of it. We have special tutors to help you. My particular responsibility is to ensure that you are thoroughly acquainted with the habits and friends of the man and to put you through a severe course in Church history and ritual. By the time you leave you will be Bishop Celavsky.'

Spartov had only managed to contribute a few words here and there and, after breakfast, Granky showed him the proper way to dress in his new clothes. He adjusted the crucifix so that it was pinned at the front of Spartov's chest allowing the excess chain to fall down equally at either side.

'Now I am sure that you are full of questions and we have an hour before you are to meet Dr Klein.'

'I've already met him, the sadistic cretin.'

'Hush.' Granky looked around nervously. Be careful what you say my friend. Fritz is a little peculiar in some ways, but he is a master at his job. I will tell you something of his history, but after he has finished with you I think. Now for your questions.'

'This place. I always thought it was some kind of prison. I have been given the general outline of my task but I can't quite believe it all yet.'

'Granky sighed. 'I will try to explain. The agents here never at any time numbered more than thirty. They are chosen carefully for their intelligence and unwavering allegiance to the State. One other important attribute has to be present – a strong physical resemblance to persons in positions of potential influence in countries of the Western Alliance.' Granky took a deep breath.

'The plan is audacious, if not simple. Spies in other countries are a recognised convention. Every country has spies in every other country. A big drawback to the use of spies, however, is that they are usually attached to embassies or masquerade as business men. Generally speaking, most are known to the host country which detracts somewhat from their usefulness. Foreign nationals can be persuaded or blackmailed into co-operation but the results, although satisfactory, are essentially short term. It was thought that if it was possible to substitute a thoroughly reliable Soviet agent for a man in a politically sensitive area of foreign government, the results could be both satisfactory and long term. It is vital that the operation is carried out with minimum risk and, therefore, it was decided that a fundamental part of the plan should be the substitution of young, relatively unimportant men who, nevertheless, showed signs of future success. It is basically a long-term plan but we are not impatient. The chosen victims are all men without close relatives.'

'But it must take years?'

'The length of training varies. It is never less than three years and, sometimes, as long as ten. Occasionally the agents are not used at all; either because the intended victim dies in the meantime or because it is obvious that he will not fulfil the original expectations.'

'How does Dr Klein fit into all this?'

'He ensures that, when the substitution occurs, the agents are as physically alike the victim as science can make them. Extensive plastic surgery is not used since it always leaves some tiny scars. Agents have to be basically doubles, same height, weight, colour of eyes and hair and same bone structure. They have to be within a couple of years of the right age. Dr Klein takes care of more sophisticated details such as existing scars, wounds and metabolism. Vaccines are duplicated and administered so that, so far as is humanly possible, the agent is an exact duplicate of the victim. It is unfortunate for the agent if the victim breaks a leg.' Here Granky smiled. 'In such a case Dr

Klein will see to it that the agent's leg is broken in exactly the same way. Sensitivity to certain drugs is reproduced, as is susceptibility to hay fever or colds.'

Spartov shuddered. He had the distinct impression that Dr Klein enjoyed the more unpleasant aspects of his job. 'Tell me about the rest of the complex.'

Cranky appeared not to hear. 'A comprehensive dossier is compiled on each of the chosen victims. The dossier includes full details of medical history, personal habits and characteristics and lists of friends and acquaintances. The dossier is updated monthly from information supplied by our agents abroad who do not know its purpose.' Granky paused and looked thoughtful for a moment as if uncertain whether to carry on. After about half a minute of mental deliberation accompanied by an irritating drumming on the table with his fingertips, he continued.

'The language of the victim is spoken exclusively, at first badly but gradually with greater proficiency until eventually the agent is expected to speak, literally, like a native of the country. He must have precisely the same intonation and accent as the victim. Not until and unless the language is perfect is substitution considered. Books, newspapers and radio programmes are provided, together with tape recordings of the victim speaking under various circumstances; in conversation, on the telephone and, if appropriate as in your case, on the public platform.'

'It is an appalling task.' Spartov had been listening with great attention. 'How is all this achieved?'

'One member of staff is assigned to each agent, in your case me, and it is his function to make sure that the agent is totally familiar with everything in the dossier and kept completely up-to-date with the comings and goings of the victim. The agent has to learn to act exactly as the victim would act. If the victim is well versed in history, the agent has to be equally capable, has to have read the same books and be familiar with the same radio and TV programmes and films. Sports achievements, if any, have to be duplicated. In short, the agent has to compress the whole of the victim's life into a few years of intensive study. Of course, not all parts of the victim's life are given the same weight. As time passes, memory fades. Newsreels and documentaries are shown frequently and a certain amount of play acting takes place in the appropriate parts of the sets which you may have noticed built in the grounds.'

'Familiarity with foreign restaurants, taxis and homes is an essential ingredient, much more of course. The agent's life is hard and unremitting. Relaxation is confined to forms of relaxation enjoyed by the intended victim. An evening at the theatre, films or a visit to a restaurant with some of the language staff, who are intent upon trapping him into making a mistake. After the first stage is over – a full knowledge of the victim's habits, friends and language – the agent is fully occupied in constantly updating his knowledge.'

'Spartov was astounded. He was speechless for a moment. 'Is it permissible to ask how many agents have been placed?' Granky had gone to get himself a drink from the kitchen.' I don't see why not,' he called. 'Twelve agents have been placed in important departments in foreign countries. Two of them, I may say, are now in very high positions, sending much useful information back to us. Fifteen agents are in the complex at present.' Granky finished his drink, it might have been water or vodka, and looked at his watch. 'Now we must call on Dr Klein.'

***

'Spartov lay, half reclining, on a leather couch. Klein studied him with rapidly blinking eyes. Huge blow-ups of Celavsky's face were taped to the walls of the small, white-painted surgery. An assistant hovered near. Klein peered more closely, favouring Spartov with a whiff of malodorous breath. Spartov winced and Klein moved back. He picked up a clipboard and ran down a list. Glancing at Spartov as at a cadaver on a slab, he assumed what he regarded as his best professional manner.

'We shall need to give attention to the ears. They require tying back, and to the eyebrows. Perhaps also, yes, a little correction to the hairline. Everything else appears to be precisely right.' Klein seemed genuinely sorry.

'We will commence your treatment tomorrow. Take no food or drink except water from now until then as I have to use a general anaesthetic.' Again, the note of regret. He smiled suddenly. 'You will suffer considerable amount of pain afterwards until the wounds are healed.'

Spartov was glad to leave the white and chrome world of the unpleasant doctor.

In the event, Spartov felt little pain although his imagination of pain to come had more than made up for that. After four weeks under the loving care of Dr. Klein, Spartov was discharged to take up his serious study. He fervently hoped that Bishop Celavsky took care of himself.

Thursday 25 May 1978

During the years that followed Spartov's rather abrupt introduction into the Linanka, he found his time split more or less evenly, between languages, theology and Celavsky himself. By means of photographs and films, he became well acquainted with the appearance and names of all Celavsky's colleagues.

Bishop Celavsky, it seemed, was a strong sports-loving man, well liked but firm in his dealings with his people. He was much given to long walks in the hills and he was an outspoken critic of communism. He was a nuisance and an embarrassment to the Czech government. He was so beloved by the people of his diocese, however, particularly the young, that it was exceedingly difficult to move against him openly.

Spartov sat in his room, with the day's Czechoslovak newspaper half read in his lap. He twiddled with the episcopal ring on his finger and wondered if he would ever get the opportunity to take over the role of Celavsky, who by this time had been transferred to Prague as Archbishop and received the red hat which meant that he was a cardinal.

Meanwhile, events were moving on.

3. ARTHUR

6 June 1978

A small bald-headed man sat in a bachelor apartment, part of a Georgian Terrace of the more ambitious kind, in the area to the south of Buckingham Palace. The furnishings were opulent, deep pile carpets, tan leather armchairs and original modern paintings on the walls. Wine coloured velvet curtains at the windows hung all the way down to the floor. Outside, the June morning was clear and mild.

The bald-headed man was not thinking of the flat and its elegant appointments, nor the weather. As he leaned over the antique French escritoire shuffling a stack of files, his mind was far away. It was essential that he chose carefully. He looked through the files again. He had reduced them to five: Maurice Rousseau, Lia Otello, Rex Carter, Otto Lentz and Genero Picca.

He finally put two files aside and addressed large brown paper envelopes to the remaining three. A brief note was penned to each and tucked into the appropriate envelope, then he put them away in a drawer, locked it and picked up the telephone in his long slender fingers. His first calls were to the airport to book three tickets. After the transaction was completed to his satisfaction, he rang his bank and arranged for several thousand pounds to be available, in various currencies, later in the day. At length he was satisfied and poured himself a generous measure of whisky. He relaxed in an armchair near the bookcase, cradling his drink. He stroked the bindings lovingly. It had been six months since the idea had first come to him and he had spent the time refining his scheme and, most important, gathering information about possible associates.

He went for lunch to his club and sat for an hour afterwards reading the day's papers. His next call was at his bank, where the manager received him as a valued customer and handed over the money as requested. From there, he went to the terminal building at Heathrow, picked up three airline tickets and returned home. There, he transferred the tickets and appropriate sums of money into each of the three envelopes, had a simple evening meal then set off again to a performance of 'La Traviata' at Covent Garden with a youthful Placido Domingo in the principal role. He posted the envelopes on the way. He enjoyed the opera immensely and got home late after supper alone at a small Italian restaurant where he was a regular patron. He went to bed and fell into a dreamless sleep.

Tuesday 4 July 1978

Warm fingers of rain beat on the windscreen of the taxi as it drew up in a quiet street, not far from London's Notting Hill. A small lake of water swirled over the pavement provoking none too friendly glances from the few varicoloured pedestrians who scurried on their bedraggled ways. The taxi driver accepted his fair from the solitary occupant and sped off into the night.

Maurice Rousseau straightened up, feeling the water trickling down the back of his neck, he approached the crumbling façade of the hotel. Had the neon sign been working properly, it would not have proclaimed 'EXCELSIO OTEL'; but it was not and it did. The desk clerk, dry as the night outside was wet, looked up from his paper without interest. He cocked a greasy thumb in the direction of the stairs at the back of the narrow hall in answer to Rousseau's query.

Rousseau went up to the first floor quickly and found room 14 without difficulty. He knocked twice and waited. The door was opened and he found himself in a small room, thick with cigarette smoke. Glasses and an opened bottle of whisky stood on a table around which were arranged four chairs. Two were occupied, the man who opened the door sat on a third and motioned Maurice to sit in the remaining vacant place. Apart from the table and chairs, the room had no furniture. The décor was in various tints of brown which probably owed more to cigarette smoke than to the decorator's art. The faded curtains were tightly drawn to keep out the July air and pinned together. The heat was oppressive.

The little man with the bald head, who had been sitting at one end of the table toying with a glass was the first to speak. 'Good to see you. Maurice Rousseau, I presume?' 'Yes.' Maurice was just a trifle impatient. He had received a package containing an airline ticket from France to London, directions to the Excelsior Hotel, two thousand new franc notes and the cryptic letter that informed him that it would be to his advantage to be at room 14 at nine o'clock. Being a gambler as well as a thief and having nothing to fear from the authorities in England, he had taken little time to decide to accept the strange invitation. He was intrigued, to say the least. He was now even more puzzled. The bald man, about fifty by the look of him, had the appearance of a clerk in a small office. To his left was a tall blond young man, rather Swedish in appearance, but that might just be his fair hair colouring, who sat steadily smoking. He had opened the door. In his open-necked blue shirt and jeans he looked fresh out of college.

But, by far the most interesting of his new companions was the raven-haired woman of indeterminate age, as all women who are past their first youth should be. She perched on the right of the bald man and slightly away from the pool of bright light immediately under the old-fashioned brass light fitting. He guessed she was nearer forty than thirty, but she was strikingly beautiful. She was dressed in black and smiled at him slightly. The bald man, having given time for Maurice to take in his surroundings, such as they were, and look at his companions, spoke again. Maurice was struck by the strangeness of his voice, which was soft and liquid.

'Thank you for coming, all of you. You must be bursting with questions but may I ask you to save them until I have finished and then you can ask whatever you like?' The bald man had a curiously old-fashioned way of shaping his sentences which made him seem even more like a clerk in a small office. He had, in fact, carefully rehearsed his little speech. He knew it would be the most important speech of his life. The others nodded, but said nothing, waiting.

None of you, so far as I am aware, has ever met before. Neither have I met any of you before tonight, although I know a good deal about you.' He paused and looked faintly embarrassed as if he had just peeked, ever so slyly, at an unopened Christmas present.

First of all, my name is Arthur Brown. Yes, it is, really.' They looked unconvinced. 'Just one stage removed from John Smith eh? Well, never mind that.

On my left is Rex Carter,' indicating the blond young man. 'The gentleman who has just joined us is Maurice Rousseau and this young lady here is Miss, or should I say Signorina, Lia Otello. I have invited you all to join me to put to you a little proposition which will provide a great deal of money for all of us.'

It was as if an electric charge had been introduced among the tobacco fumes in the air. Maurice began picking at the shredded skin around his finger nails. Lia's eyes widened and she ran the tip of her tongue along her lips in a faintly erotic way. Rex Carter leaned forward in his chair. Arthur smiled an inward smile of gratification.'

'Let me tell you a little about yourselves. Rex, you are somewhat older than your appearance suggests. You have taken part in armed robberies and at least two killings. You did the killing with the knife that you always keep concealed in your shirt.' Rex made a small movement and looked around like a cat among dogs. Arthur Brown ignored him and turned to the Frenchman.

'Maurice, you are extremely successful, in a small way, in France as a confidence trickster. But for your fondness for the ponies, you would be a rich man today most likely.' It was Maurice's turn to look uncomfortable. His craggy face turned a shade paler under his red hair. If you set your mind to the task, I imagine that you could easily sell us the hotel we are sitting in.' Arthur smiled as though encouraging the other to do just that. Maurice looked rather older than Arthur expected. He knew Maurice was only thirty-seven but he could easily have passed for a man ten years older, part of his success perhaps? Since it looked as though Maurice had declined the challenge, Arthur continued.

'Last but by no means least, Lia.' Arthur had intended a friendly smile but succeeded instead in producing a slimy leer. 'You started in prostitution in Naples and quickly left that behind to run several rackets in Rome. We need not go into details but, suffice to say, you know Rome and its ways like the back of your hand; rather better actually. All of you are vital to my little scheme. None of you, amazingly, has a police record. You would be of no use if you had. Now for myself.' He lowered his eyes modestly, as if half afraid to present his curriculum vitae to such a distinguished gathering of talent.

'I am a man of private means. How I got those "means" is unimportant, but I, too, have no police record. I have very efficient means of finding out what I need to know, as I hope I have just demonstrated. My little schemes have netted me, in the past, a substantial income. However, we all dream of being able to retire to a life of ultimate luxury and I am no exception. On the other hand, at my time of life, I have no intention of tasting the inside of Her Majesty's prisons for the first time. My little project will ensure that we can all indulge our most expensive fantasies for the rest of our lives.' Arthur was still speaking quietly, calmly almost gently, but strong emotions clearly lurked just below the surface and the pores of his face were releasing tiny drops of moisture in silent witness.

'I doubt that even you, Maurice, are capable of giving sufficient away to the gentlemen of the turf to prevent you enjoying total luxury. In brief my proposition, if you are agreeable, although fraught with some danger – what isn't? – will produce just as much money as you want.' He paused and looked around with pleasure at the stunned expressions on three faces.

'How do we know that you are not trying to sell us something or set us up for that matter?' It was Maurice who spoke. 'How do I know that the three of you are not in this together?' He edged his chair a little further back from the table.

The bald man adopted a patient attitude as if addressing a backward child. 'Firstly. There is no question of any of us being in league with the others against you. None of us have ever met before. Also, consider that none of you have sufficient money to make these elaborate precautions worthwhile. Remember, I sent each of you a sum of money and your travel ticket to enable you to reach here. If any of you are not convinced, you are free to leave now and you may keep the money already given to you. It would be a great pity, however, because each of you has been chosen especially, to play a particular part in the scheme. If it will convince you further, let me say that I intend to finance the operation entirely from my own funds. None of you is being asked to contribute anything more than your time and talents.' Arthur Brown looked directly at Maurice, who noticed, for the first time, that there was a hard glint behind Arthur's eyes which belied the smooth roundness of his face.

'Well, if it is a confidence trick, it's got some new angle I never thought of.' Maurice relaxed a little. Lia and Rex had said nothing but stared fixedly at Maurice, seemingly prepared to follow his lead.

'Now before I outline details of my scheme.' Arthur had obviously decided that the objections had been overcome. 'Before we proceed to the interesting part, I must ask you all whether you wish to participate or not. If not, please leave now. You have just a few minutes to decide and I must warn you that there will be danger involved and several months of boredom before the scheme can come to fruition.'

'How many months of boredom?' asked Rex. Arthur looked annoyed for a moment and favoured Rex with a speculative glance. 'It's extremely difficult to say with any precision. Perhaps six months, but what is that set against the prize?'

Lia spoke for the first time. 'You must be aware that my rackets, as you are pleased to describe them, are not prospering. They are a living, that is all. That is why I have flown over. Had my own businesses been thriving you could not have enticed me to join you from Roma. I wish to be included.' Arthur looked less than happy with her qualified acceptance and pouted slightly.

'Count me in.' Rex was brief and to the point. He never wasted words. His face remained expressionless and no trace of his thoughts could be read through his duck egg blue eyes. His thoughts were not, as a matter of fact, very profound. He simple saw this as yet another job. He was being hired, possibly to kill; it made no difference, provided the pay was good, and it sounded good. He was a completely amoral animal. His mind was quick and his movements slow and deliberate. He liked danger for its own sake as something to overcome. Danger was his life, sex his relaxation.

Arthur turned to Maurice. 'Well?'

'Yes, your offer of untold wealth naturally appeals to me.'

'Good.' Arthur rubbed his hands together. They all noticed the unusually slim fingers, almost like a woman's. Maurice wondered if Arthur was homosexual, not that he cared either way. Arthur would have to get up early to put anything over on Maurice Rousseau. He would be on his guard every moment. Not that it had helped two years ago during the affair in the Rue Marchande, but he preferred to forget that particular episode. He had got out of it by the skin of his teeth. He wondered if Arthur knew about it…. probably.

Arthur was not unaware of the thoughts and motives which lay behind the acceptance of his proposition, even before they had heard any details. They all needed money desperately. He had thoroughly vetted them all, otherwise they would not be there. The next part of the proceedings would be more difficult; to persuade them that they could carry out his scheme.

'I am not a greedy man. I propose that I should take ten per cent of the proceeds to cover all overheads and acknowledge my position as instigator of the project. The remainder to be shared equally among the four of us. I guarantee your individual shares will be not less than two million Stirling and probably very much more.' Lia gasped and smiled, not pleasantly, showing large white teeth. Little drops of moisture flecked her lips. 'Gracious,' thought Maurice. 'She's actually salivating at the prospect of money,' not that he himself was unhappy about it. He just could not grasp it and, if the sweat on his brow was any indication, Rex was struggling mightily to remain impassive.

Arthur was pleased with the reaction although, as he looked around their laboured faces, he began to feel like a bitch on heat. Would they actually tear him to pieces to find the money, he wondered? Banishing such absurd notions, he put his hands on the table, one on the other.

'It must be clearly understood that, in order to achieve success, my instructions must be obeyed exactly although I shall expect you all to offer such advice as you feel appropriate. My decision, however, must be final – agreed?'

The two men nodded. 'Yes, yes,' hissed Lia between white teeth, quite overcome by anticipation.

'Good. Put quite simply, my plan is to carry out a kidnapping and collect the ransom.'

The atmosphere in the room was similar to squeezing a wet sponge over a pile of heated coals. The adrenalin pump suddenly stopped pumping and went into reverse. Lia looked as though she could not believe her ears. Dismay, frustration and finally anger chased each other across her symmetrical features. Maurice felt suddenly tired and wanted to go home. Unexpectedly, it was Rex who voiced their feelings.

'You stupid bastard, you brought us...' He got no further, the chair leg was expertly hooked from under him and he toppled back onto the worn carpet, vainly clutching at his shirt. He struggled into a sitting position on the floor to find himself staring at the business end of a small automatic, complete with silencer, held quite unwaveringly in Arthur's left hand. It had appeared as if by magic.

'I do not appreciate your sentiments Rex. If you make one move for your knife, you are dead. Get up and sit down properly like a good boy and listen.' The young killer sent spears of hate at Arthur but he got up without a word, righted the chair and sat down sullenly. Maurice was still trying to figure out where the gun had come from. Lia shot a look of open admiration at Arthur.

Arthur smiled, 'I probably neglected to mention that I am extremely experienced in the art of gunfighting. But enough of that, I am perfectly well aware that in bald terms, my project may appear to be unoriginal, to put it mildly. If any of you still think I am a fool, go now.' He put his gun inside his coat and replaced his hands on the table. No one moved except Maurice, who poured himself a drink.

'Let us understand why previous attempts at kidnapping show such a high proportion of failures. Firstly, choice of victim, the standard kidnapper often misjudges his victim's ability or willingness to command the appropriate amount of money. So, instead of having a valuable saleable commodity, he has a liability on his hands. Secondly, the holding of the kidnap victim is not sufficiently safe and, within a few days, he finds himself with his victim surrounded by police. Lastly, the arrangement for paying the ransom are often too pathetic for words. You will notice that very few kidnaps actually fail at the important point, securing the victim.' He paused and poured them all a drink. Without exception, they all listened intently. There was a feeling that something quite unique was about to be revealed.

'I have a fairly good idea of the premises I need to hold the victim. Lia will help there. The payment of the ransom is also carefully considered, so as to be fool proof. The actual kidnapping will be the most difficult part in this case, but Maurice, I have faith that you will pull it off for us, with assistance of course. That part, also, is carefully planned. Lastly, the victim. Someone, for whom, not one but millions will put up the ransom money, for whom the involvement of police and massive publicity will assist not hinder us.' He took out from his wallet four tickets to Rome.

Rex looked blank, Lia was clearly frightened. Maurice began to understand.

4. ARRIVALS

Sunday 30 July 1978

Arthur arrived in Rome courtesy of Alitalia Airlines. He checked into his hotel under his own name, one of the perks of having no police record, and spent the remainder of the day carefully sorting his belongings into neat and orderly arrangements in drawers and wardrobe, ready for a long stay.

Monday 31 July 1978

Before Maurice arrived by train from Paris, Arthur telephoned Lia and learned that she had located a suitable apartment for the operation. He arranged to look at it with her after the siesta. He did not see Maurice that day.

Tuesday 1 August 1978

Arthur saw Maurice across the restaurant at breakfast. Three out of four, so far so good. That only left Rex to complete the party and he was due to arrive in a few hours, having flown to Pisa and taken the train to Rome. There was nothing to connect them, three tourists, two English and one French. Arthur positioned himself in the entrance lounge of the hotel and saw Rex arrive. If Arthur epitomised the typical English traveller abroad with his numerous suitcases and capacious trunk, Rex looked the typical student in sweat shirt, jeans and duffle bag. That young man will have to be carefully watched, thought Arthur as he busied himself with 'Osservatore Romano'. He felt excited and elated as he always did at the start of a new venture.

All his plans were laid. So far, admittedly, they were only at the beginning but, so far, everything had progressed smoothly. There would necessarily be a period of familiarisation. It was important to get to know certain parts of Rome quite well so that there would be no bungles. He felt very pleased with himself that day.

5. DEATHS

Sunday 6 August 1978

Pope Paul VI had died of a massive heart attack. Crowds gathered pointlessly in the piazza outside the summer residence of the popes at Castel Gandolfo some 24 kilometres from Rome. They prayed or they wept; others simply gaped at the shuttered windows and took flash photographs for family albums.

It was cooler than in Rome, but it was still hot. The evening sun clung desperately to the sky before dropping suddenly out of sight behind the Alban hills. Then it was dark as if to emphasise that the Roman Catholic Church appeared to be temporarily, leaderless.

The organisation of the Roman Catholic Church is a complicated affair, composed of sacred congregations, dicasteries, secretariats, and special offices. A curious appointment, is that of Camerlengo of the Holy Roman Church. This prelate assumes responsibility for the continued functioning of the Church in the interval between the death of one pope and the election of his successor. He also carries out the curious, though ancient, process of verifying the pope's death by tapping the pope's forehead with a silver hammer while calling out his baptismal name three times followed by the breaking of the pope's ring and papal seal. The occupant of this office on that August evening was His Eminence Giusseppi Cardinal Bangio. Cardinal Bangio started to be very busy indeed.

The next three weeks until the election of Albino Luciani as Pope John Paul I were hectic. Cardinal Electors gathered in Rome from all over the world. Purple-robed dignitaries abounded, some old and holy, some old and dynamic, some just old.

'Thank God it will be many years before we have to go through this again.' It was one of Cardinal Bangio's less fortunate statements.

6. MAURICE MAKES A FRIEND

Friday 29 September 1978.

Arthur Brown sat in his hotel bedroom near the Piazza della Repubblica. The low block of the huge Rome railway station in the middle distance sat blankly among the old buildings like a huge flat book dropped haphazardly by Mussolini's clumsy fist. The sunlight glinted on the long white entrance canopy. In the piazza below, hundreds of Italians were clearly bent upon killing each other in an assortment of cars, trucks and scooters, which whizzed around the spacious central fountain. The old Baths of Diocletian, partly converted by Michelangelo to a church for the use of the Catholic Church, presented a fittingly expressionless exterior to the traffic and station alike, from which it was separated by a pleasant stretch of garden.

Arthur sat at the small table looking at this animated scene, but he was not appreciating it. 'Damn,' he said to no one in particular. In the background, as if to underline his depression, the radio was interrupted yet again by a solemn voice proclaiming: 'Il Papa è morto.' 'Damn him,' he implored. Although whether his remark referred to the announcer or 'Il Papa' himself was not clear. 'Damn him to hell,' he elaborated on the destination as if to make his plea perfectly comprehensible to whoever might be inclined to act upon it.

Arthur laid his mother-of-pearl customised Waterman writing instrument carefully on the notepad, making sure that its lines were parallel to the edge of the paper. Then he got up and lay gently on the bed to gather his thoughts. The room was typical of cheap hotel bedrooms throughout Rome. Slightly overlarge furniture of old fashioned vintage stood on the multi-hued terrazzo floor. Cream washed walls reflected the evening light glinting from well-designed yellow metal wall fitments, door handles and light switches.

The only other occupant of the room was Maurice Rousseau. 'Cheer up Arthur,' he said, eyeing the other with some trepidation. 'I can't help it Maurice. Two popes in less than two months. Is this what they mean by Divine intervention?' 'I doubt it' said Maurice. 'There will be another pope in three weeks and we can carry on as before.' 'But we can't, that's just the point,' said Arthur. 'My plan was carefully worked out on the basis of the known habits of Paul VI. Then I had to amend it to deal with John Paul I, except that he hadn't time to make "known habits" and now he's gone. I don't think you realise, Maurice, just how much nervous energy I use.' Arthur, dabbing his shiny head with a large coloured handkerchief, had patently lost his characteristic calm. His liquid voice, rising in pitch, had acquired a certain disagreeable viscosity. 'I think I'll just have a rest. Come and see me tomorrow.'

Maurice took the elaborate lift to the ground floor and went out into the evening sunlight. He started to walk down the broad Via Nazionale past the smart shops and smarter offices cunningly integrated into the ancient fabric of the buildings. The city was unbelievably busy with traffic and pedestrians. Maurice kept to the centre of the pavement. Experience told him that it was the one area likely to give unimpeded progress. Along the wall side, people tended to loiter, staring in shop windows, standing in doorways or just standing for no apparent reason. The same sort of thing happened at the outer third of the pavement width, the third near the kerb. Dogs, people waiting to cross the road, people who had just crossed, bus queues and business men waiting for taxis; a pavement was just like a river, the debris accumulated near the banks. Maurice owed his livelihood to putting comparatively simple observations of this kind to work. He was, he had to be, a student of human beings in just the same way as some people studied the behaviour of rats or monkeys. Maurice would probably have continued his obsessive study even if there had been no money in it. In fact, there was plenty.

During the past nine weeks stay in Rome, Arthur had been continually frustrated, Rex had been bored and Lia had simply gone about her usual business, but Maurice had applied his mind to the task of gaining the friendship of Francesco Sarto, the Pope's principal chauffer. Arthur had not said why Maurice should do this but, apparently, it was vital to the plan. Arthur had supplied the name from his own intelligence network, which seemed to be as vague as it was obviously comprehensive. Sarto was the chief of three chauffeurs, forty years old and married with five children. He lived in the section of the Vatican known as the village. There were few permanent laymen or women resident in the Vatican City, in fact, even including cardinals, the total residents numbered only about seven hundred and fifty, but Sarto was one of them so that he could always be available if required.

Sarto was in the habit of taking an evening glass of wine in a trattoria in the tangle of streets between the Vatican and the Castell S. Angelo. Maurice had already scraped an acquaintance and had given Sarto to understand that he was semi-permanently in Rome, representing a French newspaper. He made his way to the trattoria now in leisurely fashion.

It was eight o'clock when he arrived and, shunning the pavement tables, he made his way inside. The café was almost empty. An American couple of mature years sat in a tangle of guide books and photographic impedimenta at a table near the window and talked in that curiously loud way endemic in the American abroad, at home too for all Maurice knew. An aged Italian sat near the bar engaging the proprietor in what sounded like an argument to the death. The empty tables would soon fill up and Maurice settled himself where he could observe the passing scene outside. He was nearly through his second plate of spaghetti, liberally sprinkled with parmesan cheese of which he was inordinately fond, when Sarto came in, saw Maurice with obvious delight and sat down at his table.

'What a day this has been, eh Maurice my friend?' Normally an amiable man, today Sarto was subdued. His eyes were red-rimmed. He was small and compact, neatly groomed with black hair carefully combed and greased and a small Hitler moustache.

'This will have hit you very hard, Francesco.'

'He was such a nice man, a good man.' Sarto seemed on the verge of breaking into tears and Maurice quickly ordered a carafe of Frascati. The wine restored the chauffer's spirits somewhat and he grew confidential. 'Do you know he spoke to me about my family just as we are doing now. He always asked if I would mind driving him. If I would mind! He would have been a very great Pope. He was a very great Pope. I could not believe it when I heard the news.'

Maurice shifted slightly in his chair. 'I'm sure you will be happy with your new master, whoever that turns out the be.'

'Yes, the Holy Spirit will provide another great man, but it is all so distressing.' Sarto lapsed into silence, staring glumly at his drink apparently not sure that the Holy Spirit was equal to the task. He roused himself after a few minutes of uncomfortable silence. 'You will have been busy today, Maurice, with reports for your paper in France I'm sure.'

The café had filled with people, Maurice had finished his late meal and suggested that it was time to leave. He proposed walking back with Sarto to the Vatican. They parted at St Ann's Gate. Sarto gripped his arm. 'I will see you again, I hope?'

'Certainly. I will be around for an indefinite time.'

'The next time we meet, well perhaps not then but in a few weeks' time when things are less busy inside, you must let me show you around the Vatican City. You cannot get in by yourself but I will vouch for you.'

'That would be a real delight,' said Maurice and meant it. 'Thank you very much.' The Italian's face glowed with pleasure and they separated on the understanding that they would meet regularly to drink a glass of wine and chat. Sarto seemed to have few friends although, to judge by the many 'buena seras' exchanged as they stood in the shadow of the city walls, many acquaintances.

It was midnight when Maurice arrived back at the hotel where he had a room on the floor below Arthur and above Rex. They had arrived separately and kept up the pretence that they did not know each other for the benefit of the hotel staff. Maurice was tired and decided that a report on his latest meeting with Sarto could wait until the next day.

7. CONCLAVE

Friday, 20th October 1978

Even as the cardinals filed into the conclave area of the Vatican to choose a successor to John Paul I, the shock of his sudden death had not been absorbed fully by the Vatican staff. His private secretary, who had served two popes, had declared his intention to ask to be released from his duties. An atmosphere of intense gloom pervaded the city. Dark clouds sat heavily in the sky.

The period between the death of the Pope and the Conclave to elect his successor is referred to as 'Sede Vacante'(Vacant Seat or See). All the most important business of the Church was carried on by the Camerlengo, his assistants and the cardinals heading various departments. During the actual Conclave itself, which took place in a sealed off portion of the Vatican Palace which housed the Sistine Chapel where the actual voting took place, the usual dignified bustle of the congregations, tribunals and offices fell into a kind of slow time. Everything waited. It had been known for the election of a new Pope to take months or, in some bizarre cases, even years but, thanks to some reorganisation of the methods of voting, recent elections had been counted in days from the start of the actual Conclave. Meanwhile, in-trays overflowed with letters and reports. Some trivial items could be dealt with but no letters of any importance were issued for three weeks. The world's press and a sizeable percentage of the Roman population haunted Bernini's vast piazza in front of the basilica, taking bets on the colour of the smoke issuing from the makeshift chimney.

When undeniably white, or to be more accurate pale grey, smoke made its appearance at the end of the fourth ballot on the second day of the Conclave, the mad rush to the piazza really began. Every available vantage point was filled as arc lights trained upon the central balcony, augmenting the floodlights on the main façade of the basilica.

It was almost dark. The babbling crowd suddenly hushed as if someone had turned down the volume switch as the tall glass doors opened and a figure bearing a tall golden cross came into view. Wild applause rang out. Tingles ran down tens of thousands of stretching spines in the square and millions more who watched on TV. Technicians cursed as they fought last minute hitches, commentators fumbled with sheaves of papers detailing the names and careers of the most likely of the one hundred and twenty cardinals to be elected.

A tiny group had assembled on the balcony. The figure of the senior Cardinal Deacon stood clutching a piece of paper while a priest held the book in readiness for the Apostolic Blessing to be given by the new Pope and a further priest held a stick microphone towards the Cardinal Deacon who took a rather nervous breath.

'Annuntio Vobis gaudium magnum, habemus Papem *(I bring you tidings of great joy, we have a Pope).*' The crowd in St Peter's Piazza applauded and the elderly Cardinal peered cautiously at the scrap of paper in his hand: 'Eminentissimum ac Reverendissimum Dominum Wenceslas Tadeo Sanctae Romanae Ecclesiae Cardinalem Celavsky *(Most Eminent and Most Reverend Lord Wenceslas Tadeo Cardinal of the Holy Roman Church Celavsky).*'

Utter silence in the piazza, then confusion, surprise, finally the dawn of understanding and delight. Radio and TV commentators croaked incomprehensively into their microphones as they frantically searched for the unexpected name among their cards. The Cardinal Deacon had not finished: 'qui sibi nomen imposuit *(Who has taken the name)* Leo XIV'. Thunderous applause, cheering and clapping burst out all over the vast piazza as a broad-shouldered athletic figure moved forward into the brilliant light, climbing the three steps which brought him within full view of the crowd. The white soutane, one of three of different sizes prepared in advance, visibly strained across his chest. The sound of the Swiss Guard presenting arms in the piazza below was lost in the sheer volume of sound.

The hush returned as the Pope raised his hands. In a slightly accented Italian he paid tribute to his predecessor and to the nineteenth century Pope Leo who was the author of the great worker's charter Rerum Novarum concerning the rights and duties of capital and labour.

In all corners of the world, the election of Pope Leo XIV, the first non-Italian Pope for four centuries, was greeted with amazement. 'Vatican Watchers' were hustled in front of TV cameras only to admit, slowly and at great length, to the viewing public that they knew practically nothing about the new Pope, beyond the fact that he was Czechoslovakian and an enemy of communism who had fought it at first hand. A well-known news channel produced a potential scoop in the form of a Czechoslovak priest who had known the new Pope some twenty years earlier. Unfortunately, his English turned out to be so bad as to be unintelligible and the interview was swiftly terminated.

The news took longer to filter through to Iron Curtain countries, where it was greeted with undisguised pleasure by the bulk of the population and faintly disguised displeasure by their governments. In Czechoslovakia, the excitement was intense and there was, quite literally, dancing in the streets.

In the small corner office in the Linanka Complex, Major Kutznov answered the telephone summoning him to a very important meeting in the KGB central offices in Moscow.

Inside the large conference room, the atmosphere was tense. A large portrait of Brezhnev hung on one wall and frowned unreasonably at the wall opposite. As the world debated the effect of having a comparatively young Czech cardinal on the throne of Peter, five elderly bull-necked men in dark suits and one large pudding-faced man in military uniform debated the fate of Andrei Spartov.

Kutznov was of the opinion that instant liquidation was required. 'After all, we cannot substitute now.' Elderly bull-necks one and two were in complete agreement.

'Wait.' It was elderly bull-neck number three who spoke. 'If we can substitute Spartov for Celavsky, we can substitute Spartov for Leo, provided that we have the opportunity and we do it before he has become well known. We can do it with less risk than if he had remained in his own country among friends who have known him for years.' What the two-remaining bull-necks would have said will never be known. They wisely kept their opinions to themselves.

'Can you immediately commence briefing Spartov on his new role?' Kutznov nodded in disbelief. He finally found words and hurriedly revised his earlier view. 'There is no problem. In many ways it will be easier, as you say. They are both new to the job. Opportunity is our only problem.'

Opportunity was to be revealed the following day by the Pope's own decision.

Tuesday, 22nd October 1978

The Vatican Press Office is situated in the muddled group of buildings near the Belvedere Court. It is not usually the disseminator of startling information and rarely becomes the focus of world attention.

The day after the election of Leo XIV, they had three items of information to impart to the jostling press men and women. They were handed out to the journalists in duplicated sheets, helpfully translated into half a dozen languages.

The first item, which raised not the faintest ripple of interest except among the English present, was the appointment of Monsignor Peter Dunne to be principle private secretary to His Holiness and Prefect of the Pontifical Household. Monsignor Dunne apparently was already employed as an assistant in the private secretary's office.

Next was the announcement that the Pope intended to make a special visit to his home country as soon as it could be arranged. The Press Officer on duty could or would not elaborate on the announcement except to say that it would be, of course, a purely pastoral visit, not political. This statement was greeted with scepticism by those who knew of the Pope's past struggles with the communist authorities in Czechoslovakia. It was greeted with something close to panic by members of the Press Corps from the Soviet Block

The third item concerned a Synod of the world's bishops in Rome in the New Year. Great things were expected and all the Christian Churches were invited to send participants. The world's Press gave a collective yawn.

The Press Office made no comment, they did not even hint at an unusual incident which had occurred the previous evening. It was quite unconnected with the Pope's decision to go to Czechoslovakia.

***

Peter Dunne was unsure of the wisdom of the decision. It was one thing to be decisive and quite another to be impetuous. He had the feeling that Leo was being impetuous. He readily admitted that he had nothing, other than the decision itself, on which to base such an assumption. It was equally clear that it was his duty to carry out the instructions of the Supreme Pontiff. Should he not, ought he not to speak up if he thought there was something to be said? He would have to take the matter up with his old friend the newly appointed Eminence Giorgio Cardinal Carelli. The trouble was, the new Pope had a very decisive personality, that much he had found out already. Peter put out the light and turned on his side away from the window through which came the glow of the floodlighting which illuminated St Peter's. His window opened into the San Damaso courtyard, but the light bounced off one honey-coloured stone wall onto another finally, as if by careful contrivance, focussing into Peter's new bedroom. He wondered if he would get some thick curtains put up. But he liked to see the early morning light streaming through the window almost as much as he disliked the floodlighting.

Peter was forty-five, but with his dark hair only slightly thinning at the crown, he looked younger. Above average height, he stooped somewhat from long hours working at his desk. Since his first arrival in Rome to study at the Beda College for late vocations some twenty years earlier, he had determined to spend the rest of his life there if he could manage it. His friendship with the then Monsignor Giorgio Carelli at the Vatican Secretariat of State had provided the key. Peter was not especially ambitious, but very scrupulous. So, although enthusiastic, he tended to be indecisive.

While he stared at the shifting patterns on the wallpaper on that second evening of the new Pontificate, he had difficulty in sorting out the confused emotions in his brain. Without warning, he had been summoned to the papal study about nine o'clock the previous evening. The cardinals had gone away to celebrate or commiserate with each other as appropriate. The Swiss guard on the door had let him in without a word. The Pope had been sitting behind the simple old-fashioned desk with angle poise lamp and informed him of his appointment without preamble. He had told Peter of his intention to visit Czechoslovakia and his plans for the Synod. Peter was just beginning to absorb the import of what was said when Leo had instructed him to be at the papal garage in half an hour.

If the beginning of the evening was to be engraved on Peter's memory, the latter half was to be more startling. He had arrived at the pontifical garage on the north side of the Cortile del Belvedere. The Pope emerged from a private lift dressed in the black soutane of an ordinary priest. There followed a brief ride in the black papal car, without escort, to a Roman hospital to visit an ailing bishop who, it transpired, was an old friend of the Pope. The Roman populace and the thousands of tourists thronging the streets scarcely gave the large black Mercedes, with darkened rear windows, a second look. A second look might have revealed the secret to the discerning, for the number plates were unequivocally papal – gold characters on a silver plate proclaiming 'SCV1', Stato della Citta del Vaticano. Few people could have seriously imagined that the Pope would leave the Vatican on the evening of his election. The Italian police would have been horrified, indeed a protest was lodged the next day, because the safety of the Pontiff was their responsibility while he was on

Italian soil. The hospital had evidently been alerted and they were whisked through to the Bishop's private ward without fuss. Some thirty minutes later, they were on their way back. Peter was to become used to such trips, made at all times of day and the Press were to remember the Pontificate as a running battle of wits in attempts to guess the time and place of such visits. A battle the Press seldom won.

Peter pulled the blankets over his head in an attempt to shut out the relentless golden glow and eventually fell into a dream-filled sleep, in which his father and mother were suddenly visited by the Pope. His mother fell to her knees, sinking lower and lower until she finally disappeared altogether. His father flicked on and off like a faulty fluorescent tube. A large black Mercedes carried them off into bands of coloured light.

Wednesday, 23rd October 1978

It was hot in Moscow. Inside the KGB central offices, it was hot and humid. It was virtually an all-male population. Telephones rang, teleprinters clacked and grim-faced men bustled to and fro. The décor was a uniform cream and the windows of the first two storeys were protected by mild steel bars.

Two days had passed since the election of Leo. The five elderly bull-necks and one large flat-faced major sat and sweated silently into their dark suits in the midday heat. Sweat trickled over bushy eyebrows, it coursed its way inside nylon shirts ineffectively seeking escape. Large fat bottoms were stuck immovably to simulated leather seat coverings. The room was still because movement made one aware of the heat and the sweat. Even so, two of the bull-necks smoked heavily scented cigars.

'Our opportunity has come earlier than we expected.' Operation 'Pontiff' was under consideration. The room, though large was airless. The double-glazed windows could not be opened and the air conditioning had developed a fault.

'Instructions must be given to the Czech government that they are to accept the Pope's gesture and cordially invite him to spend three days in his homeland. The culmination of the tour must be in Prague and the Pope will be put up at his old residence. The substitution must take place on the evening of the last day to give the least time and opportunity for recognition of our man Spartov.' Elderly murmurs of agreement floated across the green baize covered conference table. A glance was directed at Kutznov by one of the bull-necks.

'Your man will be ready in four weeks' time.' It was a statement not a question, and recognising it as such, Kutznov could only nod and murmur agreement. 'Two men will be sent to supervise the substitution. No one else, not even the Czech government, must know of the arrangement. We will pick the men, Kutznov, they will leave tomorrow and when they return, they will be eliminated in the usual way.' A bull-neck with small steel-rimmed spectacles tapped his cigar on the large ashtray and a finger of ash dropped symbolically onto the glass. Kutznov and the others got up slowly and uncomfortably and went stickily off to their different offices.

8. SPARTOV

Thursday, 26th October 1978

It was no less hot in the Linanka complex, but a slight breeze stirred the air, oscillated the trees and made itself felt through the ventilators above the bronze-tinted windows.

Spartov was unable to appreciate the moderating effect of the breeze as he sat down in a darkened room staring at the flickering screen. He had spent the previous two days almost non-stop in the stuffy cubicle. His companion was Granky. They paused only to eat frugal meals in the dining room, then returned to the minute cinema. Spartov saw newsreels of Popes: Pius XII, John XXIII, Paul VI and John Paul I. On this particular day, however, the newsreels had been exclusively devoted to the new Pope Leo. Scenes on the evening of his election and candid shots taken the following day. The Pope greeting fellow cardinals, the Pope greeting the disabled and the Pope greeting religious leaders of every denomination. The available newsreels were few and so they were shown over and over again.

Spartov felt strange in his sparkling white soutane. His first reaction, on learning of the election of Cardinal Celavsky, was of anti-climax, bitter disappointment and a tinge of fear. When he heard from Kutznov, that the substitution was still going ahead, he cheered up considerably and, although worried about his ability to convincingly portray Pope Leo, he threw himself into the furious schedule, absorbing everything about the new role.

Friday, 27th October 1978

A week after the election, large dockets of information started to arrive. Spartov had been virtually isolated from his fellow agents since the substitution had been authorised. He sat in one of the study rooms. The cherubic features of Granky hovered half a metre above the table opposite.

'It is not absolutely clear, Holy Father,' Granky adhered firmly to the practice of accustoming his pupils to their future titles. 'It is not clear whether Leo always uses the papal "we". Generally, he does so on formal occasions, but we, no pun intended, suspect that he uses the first person singular in everyday conversation. He appears to dislike pomp and ceremony and thus endears himself to his largely simple-minded followers.' Granky smiled a cynical smile. The news media, as you will have seen, are already talking of his charisma. I suspect that will be the most difficult thing for you to project, although you have mastered his mannerisms very well over these last years.'

Spartov shifted in his seat and adjusted his white skull cap in unconscious imitation of Celavsky. 'Do we know how he behaves in private?

'Well, we have a pretty fair idea. Our sources tell us that he is much the same in public and private. Apparently, he has the knack of doing the unexpected while yet not overstepping the fine line between himself and the rest of the Vatican staff.'

Granky picked up a piece of paper from a yellow and white leather folder. 'This is his daily routine at the moment, although he is apt to vary it if the mood takes him. He rises at five-thirty and prepares to say his Mass in his private chapel an hour later. He doesn't leave the chapel until eight-thirty, when he has breakfast alone in the dining room. After breakfast he retires to his study to attend to correspondence, speeches and scan the newspapers. Then he sees his two private secretaries, dismisses one and retains the other, Peter Dunne, who is also the prefect of the Papal Household and spends a great deal of time with the Pope, especially when the Pope meets visiting dignitaries. Then he gives audiences to visiting bishops, celebrities and anyone else who might warrant it until about half past one. Sounds like fun doesn't it? Two o'clock is lunchtime then he rests for a short time before taking the papal limousine to the Vatican gardens...'

'But according to the map you gave me, the gardens are right next to the Vatican Palace.'

'Just so; he still takes the car, presumably for security reasons. He exercises for an hour or so, sometimes walking alone or with one of his secretaries or even with a gardener. Part of this time, he reads the Divine Office from his breviary. Granky paused and turned the paper over. He continued more quickly. 'At four o'clock, or thereabouts, he returns to his dining room to take coffee. He generally changes his clothes before dinner at about seven-thirty. After dinner, he usually listens to the radio for a while before returning to his study to work on his papers, reports, speeches, letters and so on until perhaps one in the morning.' Granky looked up. 'It's a very punishing schedule. What do you think of it?'

Spartov shrugged and leaned back in his chair. Parts of his day sound very boring, but I will cope with it. No doubt I will be briefed on any particular aspect of my new life which will benefit our country.'

I'm sure that is so,' said Granky hurriedly. 'But, of course, that is out of my province. Major Kutznov will give you the final briefing.'

'Good. I can't wait to do something actually positive.' Spartov would have been his own last choice to undertake this particular mission. He hardly dared think how he would deal with day after day of idolatry and hypocrisy, play acting a part he so strongly despised; but there he would get his strength. Only he and his KGB masters would be able to enjoy the joke. He felt he might actually like his public appearances, smiling and waving to tens of thousands of stupid misguided westerners. Granky intruded on his thoughts.

'You had better take this timetable and memorize it. A couple of other things; he is to be crowned, enthroned or installed, we don't know quite which yet, next week in St Peter's Piazza. We will show you the whole telecast, of course, several times I'm afraid. He grinned broadly. 'He has made a certain Archbishop Giorgo Carelli his Secretary of State. If he doesn't make him a cardinal before you take his place, you had better do it – it's expected I'm told. Carelli's notes are here,' he tapped the leather folder. 'Leo has two private secretaries, a Monsignor Peter Dunne, an Englishman who seems to be the chief private secretary and head of the Pope's administration team and Monsignor Sylvester Rivera, an Argentinian. They are both new, so they should be no problem. Italian is the common language but sometimes meetings are held in Latin if varied nationalities are present. All the notes on the cardinals and other staff are in this envelope.'

He produced a thick envelope file. You had better get down to studying it as soon as possible. Some of these names are real tongue-twisters. How about His Eminence Gracias Cardinal Mattei y Cosimo Tanjhrui? Luckily he is in the Philippines so you won't see a lot of him.'

'With a name like that, he is certainly going to stay there,' said Spartov.

Wednesday, 1st November 1978

Kutznov sat, immovable as ever, as Spartov was shown into the office by Josef. He nodded to a chair, keeping his face under control with difficulty. The man sat opposite was, for all practical purposes, the Pope.

'The Pope will be installed on Saturday. Two weeks later, he arrives in Prague. He visits Hradec on Sunday and on to Brno on Monday, returning Monday evening to Prague. The substitution will take place during Monday evening ready for the flight back to Rome on Tuesday morning. Your initial contact at the Vatican will be our ambassador. That is all you need to know.' Kutznov lapsed into silence and pressed the button on his desk to signal dismissal.

Friday, 3rd November 1978

The little group of conspirators were crowded into Arthur's room together for the first time since they had arrived in Rome. Lia and Rex sat on the bed, Arthur in the chair by the window and Maurice sat in the armchair. Arthur was at his most unctuous.

'I know these last few weeks have been trying for all of you, but we are vastly progressed. The new Pope has shown, in the two weeks he has been in office, that he is a highly unconventional character. We know that much from the newspapers alone but Maurice here has profited from his friendship with the man Sarto. Maurice?'

'Yes, we know for example, his rough routine. I say "rough" because he varies it to suit circumstances. He is much given to slipping out of the Vatican late at night to visit prisons, hospitals and old peoples' homes.' Arthur cut in with a wave of his slim fingers.

'Thank you, Maurice, continue to cultivate Sarto and keep a record of Leo's forays. In a few weeks, they will hopefully settle into a pattern which will help us.' He turned back so that he completely faced the others. 'I must say that I viewed the election of a new Pope with trepidation. You see I had a carefully worked out plan for Paul VI, but it is fruitless to consider that now. The whole secret is to be flexible.' Arthur explained as to a class of small children. He slowly rubbed his little finger down the side of his nose. 'Lia has obtained a safe house in the Trastevere quarter of the city. The whole area is very much run down and a maze of streets. I will take up residence there from next Monday in the guise of an author who is getting on with his work. I do not foresee that I will be disturbed. Rex and Maurice, I want you both to spend some time, separately of course, thoroughly familiarising yourselves with the area between central Rome and Trastevere.'

'I've walked the streets until I've got blisters.' Rex was in a surly mood but Arthur was equal to him. 'It is essential to the scheme I have in mind that we all get to know that section of Rome thoroughly. I will explain why in my own good time. Surely it is worth a few months of gentle strolling?' Rex did not seem convinced but stared at the floor in silence.

'Such a pity you take no interest in Architecture or History, Rex,' said Arthur.

'Perhaps Lia can fix him up with someone to interest him.' Maurice smiled good naturedly at Rex who looked up briefly in annoyance. Lia smiled also, but said nothing. 'Come, come,' said Arthur, we must not have any bad feeling. When the time comes, it will be essential to work as a team.'

Maurice took out a packet of cigarettes, lit one and looked through the haze of smoke directly at Arthur. 'When do you anticipate the time will come?'

Arthur stood up and stretched, then moved closer to the window. Clearly, he was trying to come to some kind of decision. After gazing at the busy throng below for a moment, he turned back and began slowly pacing the room. Three pairs of eyes watched him. 'As you know, our plans have been changed due to two of our intended victims dying in rapid succession, most inconsiderate.' Arthur stopped pacing to smooth invisible hairs across his shiny pate.' However, such is the nature of our victim that another is always found to take his place. But it leads to complications. I require a certain period of time to take stock. The procedure I have devised for removing him from circulation is relatively simple but timing is everything. In three weeks', time, he will have returned from Czechoslovakia and we must keep our ears to the ground for a month or so afterwards. I anticipate that the operation will take place in the New Year. By that time, you will speak Italian with reasonable fluency. Let us arrange to meet again, four weeks from today at the house in Trastevere.'

Saturday, 18th November 1978

Leo's installation had been a triumph. The memories which Peter retained were of the vast crowd, at times so quiet he could close his eyes and imagine that the square was deserted, the files of assistant priests like little penguins threading their way through the crowd clutching little gold chalices; the blood red lines of cardinals, forming and reforming, double and triple rows, then slowly lining the front of the basilica behind the white-haired figure vested in gold at the altar. The day had been cool and sharp, the images vivid. That had been two weeks ago. Since then routine had settled down, if settled it could be called, to the unexpected. Peter hurried along the carpeted corridor to the papal study. To call it a corridor is misleading. It was fully six metres wide and at least as high. Semi-circular arched windows lined the right-hand wall, shedding light upon the tapestries and frescoes on the opposite wall. The sun was already up but the corridor was always cool because it faced due north. He turned the final corner. The Swiss guard, a splodge of colour in black, red and yellow, heaved himself from the wall against which he had been leaning and stood guiltily to attention. Peter gave him a wink and was rewarded with a sheepish smile. The guard was a tall young man who made Peter feel old. He probably had just arrived from some remote Swiss Canton to do his stint of duty and felt bored with the anti-climax of it all

Peter knocked on the wood-panelled door. A green light flashed in its silver mounting on the door frame and he opened the door. The Vatican, like the Church itself, was a mixture of the very old and the brand new. He had a brief mental picture of a Rococo computer spewing out sheets of Latin typescript and then he was inside the study and in the presence of the Pope. Leo was sitting at the desk and writing quickly. On the desk stood the boxes from the Secretariat of State and the Holy Office. He looked up and clear blue eyes bored into Peter's skull.

'Good morning Monsignor. You appear to be in unusually high spirits today'

'Holy Father,' Peter was aware that his face was wreathed in smiles. He walked forward and sat in the chair indicated. 'I was speculating on the strange mixture which is the Church. The ancient and traditional ceremonial, the masterpieces of Renaissance architecture and the little pieces of modern technology of which we make use.'

'Ah yes, we have come a long way since poor Galileo have we not? To keep and use that which is good of past and present, that is the secret.' Leo picked up a pile of letters and put them in a red leather box adding to it, with a flourish, a couple of small cassettes from the Dictaphone which stood to one side of the desk. He closed the box and handed it across the desk to his private secretary. Peter cradled it on his knees and put his notepad and pencil on top, waiting.

'I would prefer my entire correspondence to be with children. They are innocent and unspoiled by the world. They see more clearly than we do.'

'Just so, Holy Father.'

'Now to business. You cannot know how much I am looking forward to the visit we are to make tomorrow. I must have chance to meet old friends for what must surely be the last time.'

'I must confess that I was surprised how quickly the Czechoslovak Government responded to your intimation of a visit.'

'Where is your faith, Monsignor? All things are possible with faith. Now I want you to look at these speeches. I have drafted four. One on arrival, one for each centre we visit and one to give in Prague. I will wish to work on the last one on the last evening, in the light of our experiences during our visit. I want to say something which will be a message of hope before I leave. Perhaps you will look through them, make any amendments you see fit and let Sister Beatrice type them out so that we can go over them tonight.' He closed a folder and handed it to Peter where it joined the red box on his knee. 'Are you going to enjoy our visit do you think?'

'I am sure it will be fascinating. I have never been to Czechoslovakia.'

'It is a beautiful country with beautiful people, but suffering, I fear, from an oppressive regime. But, it will be almost a holiday for me after the events of the last month. When we come back, you will see, I will be a new man.'

9. SUBSTITUTION

Sunday, 19th November 1978

The white Alitalia DC10 with the papal coat of arms emblazoned on the side, slipped out of the sun and descended to the tarmac runway outside Prague. It took forever to descend. The multitude thronging the freshly painted airport buildings had shouted themselves hoarse long before the giant machine pulled to a halt before the red carpet and ceremonial stand. The jet scream died away and the steps were adjusted against the hull. The door opened and sore throats were once more punished, weary arms raised again as a figure in white appeared from the dark interior.

Monday, 20th November 1978

Gregor and Vladimir had never seen so many clerics in their lives. In fact, it was safe to say they had almost never seen a clergyman before. They felt vaguely uncomfortable amongst the almost tangible holiness in the episcopal residence. Officially, they were special guards and observers, sent by Mother Russia to ensure that all went well and there were no incidents to embarrass either side. As such, they had free run of the residence. They were unmistakable. Dressed in identical regulation dark brown suits and incongruous dark blue ties, they walked around the numerous corridors of the residence with measured tread. Gregor was large in every way, short black hair stood vertically from his wide forehead and a large bulbous nose seemed to blot every other feature from view. Vladimir was ugly by contrast. His eyes were set far back in his head, his nose was too thin and his mouth small and tight. Neither man smiled much. They spoke together in monosyllables as they lurked in quiet corners.

The residence had not yet claimed a new occupant but the staff were still there, specially augmented for the papal visit. The Pope had made it clear that he wanted to use his old room overlooking the small garden.

The building was three storeys high, entered straight off the pavement opposite the cathedral. It was an undistinguished square block with a central courtyard. The rear entrance faced a side street. During the last full day of the papal visit, at four o'clock in the afternoon, an elderly cleric, with a bewhiskered face and ebony stick, left a taxi a hundred yards down the road and entered the rear entrance. He was ushered up the back staircase by Gregor to a room on the first floor. Next to this room was the bedroom allocated to the Pope's private secretary and, next to that, the Pope's old bedroom.

Once inside the small bedroom, Spartov, he was the bewhiskered cleric, busied himself removing his whiskers and donning the papal soutane. A bugging device had been placed inside the papal bedroom and Spartov relaxed on the simple bed while he waited for the papal entourage to return from Brno. The contents of the room were sharply functional. Beside the bed stood a large trunk with leather straps and a small table and chair stood against the wall. On the table was a radio to receive signals from the bug and a set of headphones. A notepad and pencil were provided against the necessity for taking down particular details. It would be Spartov's duty to listen to the conversations taking place in the Pope's room so that he would be as up to date as possible when he took over. The décor of the walls was so faded as to be unclassifiable. Gregor had resumed his pacing of the corridors of the residence, alert for anything which might interfere with their preparations. Vladimir stayed in the room with Spartov.

'What time are they expected back?'

'They should be back at eight, but every phase of the tour has been running late. This Pope is very unpredictable. We should have a progress report soon from one of our agents with the tour. He doesn't know what's going on here of course.' Vladimir was using the chair back to front, sitting on it, legs astride, head resting on his arms. A black cigarette dangled from his stubby right hand. Vladimir smiled unpleasantly as if those particular muscles ached from lack of use.

'How will you do the switch?' Spartov was interested although he felt no anxiety for that part of the proceedings. He was quite sure the KGB agents would do their work perfectly.

'It will probably be better if you don't know before it happens. There will be a slight element of danger, but nothing we should not be able to handle'

At seven-thirty a triple tap, repeated twice, sounded on the door. Gregor came in. 'They have left Brno and they are headed back to Prague by helicopter.'

'Good, we can move soon,' said Vladimir.

'Not so fast,' said Gregor sharply. Spartov wondered which one was senior, probably Gregor from the way he spoke. Gregor turned to Spartov. 'The Pope has requested that the helicopter land in the grounds of the local seminary so it looks as though he intends to make a surprise visit to see the students. It is a nuisance but at least it should ensure that he is tired when he arrives back here. I should get some sleep if I were you. We will wake you the minute he gets in.'

Spartov nodded and Gregor went out again. Spartov took off the white soutane and curled up on the bed wearing only shorts. His years in the army came in useful at times like this and he was fast asleep in a few minutes. Smoke curled from the inevitable cigarette in Vladimir's hand. A little pile of stubs accumulated in the ashtray on the corner of the table. What, if anything, went through Vladimir's mind at times like this was a mystery, not to be ascertained by a study of his blank face.

Spartov was dreaming of the Kiev of his childhood when he was shaken roughly by the shoulder. He was awake immediately and felt refreshed. He swung his legs onto the floor. Vladimir, without his cigarette this time, was standing by the bed.

'Get into your things. They are just entering the building. It is just after eleven o'clock.' Spartov put on the white soutane, crucifix and skull cap for the second time that day. He was beginning to feel the adrenalin flow as he prepared for his own unique battle. As he slipped his feet into his own scarlet shoes, Vladimir continued, 'Just the Pope and his private secretary are here. The other officials are being accommodated in the papal legation. You had better take up your listening post. Let me know when the secretary leaves him.'

Spartov was already at the table and donning the headphones. Vladimir lit up again. Little specks of sweat dotted his forehead. Spartov raised a hand. 'They are entering the bedroom ... Talking about the visit to the seminary, apparently a great success... Discussing the farewell speech at the airport tomorrow.' He picked up a pencil and began to make notes.

After about an hour, during which he listened intently and Vladimir gloomily finished four more cigarettes, Spartov eased the headphones onto the back of his head and turned to the other. 'The private secretary has left.' Vladimir left the room and returned in a few minutes looking pleased with himself. 'You haven't killed him?' Vladimir shook his head. 'No, but keep listening and tell me when the Pope goes to sleep. You should be able to hear the pull switch from the bed quite clearly, we checked'

Spartov sat glued to the headphones for a further couple of hours before he finally took them off and signalled to Vladimir that the light had gone out. 'I heard the clink of a glass about five minutes before. I presume you doctored his drink also?' 'Something like that,' said Vladimir. 'We'll give him half an hour.'

Half an hour later, the two KGB men carried the large trunk out into the corridor, still brightly lit. Spartov studied his notes. They were speaking Italian together. That answers one query, he mused.

In a few minutes, the door opened once more and the KGB men entered carrying the trunk again, this time with some difficulty, 'Lucky we knew you were here, you're as alike as two twins.' Spartov gestured to the trunk which now reposed in the centre of the room. 'Is he …?'

'Yes, and quite dead. His drink was doctored with something special. We shall have no difficulty in getting this trunk back to Russia tomorrow, where the body will be examined for anything we don't know about. If anything unusual is found someone will let you know. Gregor became brisk. Our part is virtually over now. You must simply walk down the corridor and into the bedroom. We will watch the corridor at both ends. When you get into the bedroom, take off your ring and hand it through the door. You will be wearing the real thing tomorrow. Come along now, the quicker we get this part over, the better.'

'Spartov gave them a couple of minutes to get into position and then peered out into the corridor. To his right, around the corner were the service stairs he had used earlier. To his left lay two bedroom doors and, beyond, the main staircase. On the opposite side of the corridor, three doors led presumably to other bedrooms. The floor was covered in thin carpet and low wattage fitments on the wall emitted subdued lighting.

He had travelled about halfway to his destination when he heard voices on the main staircase, one was Gregor. Spartov quickened his steps. His hand was almost on the door handle when a young Czech priest appeared around the corner. He stopped in his tracks when he saw Spartov and they stared at each other for silent seconds. Then the young priest dropped to his knees. 'Holy Father, I was on my way to bed.' He indicated one of the doors on the opposite side of the corridor. 'I never imagined that you were still awake.'

'I was just reliving old memories, Father. Off to bed with you.' Spartov signed a blessing and stood waiting, smiling slightly. The priest clearly overawed, scrambled to his feet and almost dived into his bedroom. Spartov heaved a sigh of relief. It was going to be easier than he had thought. Gregor appeared from the direction of the staircase, almost literally wringing his hands. 'There was no way to stop him. I tried to delay him but he simply brushed past. Did he suspect anything?' 'Not at all,' said Spartov, confidence boosted.

The transfer passed without event and fifteen minutes later, Spartov was drifting off to sleep in the bed in which, so recently unknown to the world Leo XIV Supreme Pontiff of happy if brief memory, had died.

Tuesday, 21st November 1978

Enormous crowds lined the route to the airport. Special police had been drafted in from all the surrounding districts and, when the great white bird left the ground a collective sigh of anguish swept through the ranks of the assembled people while a sigh of relief was almost audible amongst the government dignitaries. At about the same time, a plain blue van, driven by two tough-looking men in ill-fitting brown suits, was racing with the dense traffic along the eastbound carriageway of the state autoroute; jammed between a lorry carrying frozen fish and a carload of tourists bound for the Soviet Union.

10. VATICAN

Wednesday, 22nd November 1978

So, this was the Vatican, powerhouse of the Roman Catholic Church. Spartov lay awake staring at the ceiling. Slight cracks zigzagged their way diagonally from corner to corner. It was five o'clock in the morning. He had half an hour to take stock before he would be flung into a punishing routine. It had been late when he got to bed and he had not taken everything in properly. At least, he seemed to be accepted without question which was a relief. He had had a nagging doubt that he would come across something for which he was not prepared. Fortunately, it seemed that it was the custom to guide the Pope, even around his own palace. There was always someone at his elbow to indicate, with a flourish of arm and hand, the way he was to go. Sometimes, for no obvious reason, he found himself at the end of a short procession moving from one place to another. He made a sincere, if inappropriate, prayer that Granky had forgotten nothing.

He dropped his eyes from the ceiling and looked about him. The bedroom was not at all what he had expected. Instead of thick carpets and silken drapes, his room was almost spartan, fitting in a way. A simple brass bedstead with polished knobs at the corners, plain white cotton sheets and a bare terrazzo floor not even a rug, a small bedside table which had seen better days and a straight-backed chair formed the entire furnishings. A crucifix hung above the bedstead. The walls were covered in depressing greenish flock wallpaper and darker green curtains covered the window which overlooked the courtyard of S. Damaso. His room at the complex in Linanka had been a damned sight cheerier. But then, that had been a replica of the Prague bedroom, not even the Russian agents had managed to get details of the Pope's bedroom in the Vatican. Where, he wondered, were the signs of luxury and depravity which he had been conditioned to expect? Perhaps they would come later. He got out of bed and prepared to get ready to go to his private chapel to celebrate Mass.

Three hours later, after he had had breakfast in a dining room which vied with his bedroom for the austerity prize, where the furniture was only of slightly better quality and where he had been ministered to by two black-robed, silent and aged nuns, he walked the short distance, proceeded by his chamberlain and followed by two guards, to the Pope's private study.

His study turned out to be a vast room, not at all like the impression the word 'study' conjured up in his mind. He had associated the word 'cosy' with 'study'. This room was elaborately decorated but with no sense of comfort whatsoever. He took in the chairs, the desks and the rich carpet at a glance as he passed through the doorway. He sat down behind the largest desk which was decorated in Rococo style and set near the middle of one wall. The other desks and chairs were grouped around the large desk. He sat down behind the desk and opened the box placed ready. After spending some time answering correspondence, with the help of his private secretaries, in what Granky had assured him would be suitable terms, he picked up the newspapers which were stacked in a neat pile on one corner of the desk. He spent considerable time studying the reports of Leo's visit to Czechoslovakia and his training at the Linanka complex enabled him to absorb large quantities of facts as he read through.

There was much speculation about the new Pope and revelations from 'sources close to the Vatican.' Spartov smiled. He knew that well-worn phrase covered everything from a disillusioned ex-priest to any one of the Vatican employees trading information he did not have for money he did not deserve. He roused himself and lit a cigarette from the packet on the desk. He still did not like cigarettes, but he had got past the stage of reducing the end to a wet pulp. What was the next job? Ah yes, to meet his private secretary and be briefed on the morning's appointments. There was a row of little buttons at the back of the desk, thoughtfully labelled. He pressed the one marked 'Mgr Dunne' and within a few minutes a quiet single knock and the door opposite the desk opened to admit the rather precise purposeful man he had first met in Prague only the day before.

'What appointments have you for me today, Monsignor?' pushing the leather covered box towards Peter Dunne.

Half an hour later, Spartov, swept along by a little knot of papal functionaries, found himself in the small audience chamber. Here the décor was luxurious, A throne was set on a dais at one end of the room and half a dozen or so chairs were arranged in front. The walls were hung with tapestries and the beige and white marble floor reflected the twinkling lights of the double chandeliers. A touch of informality was lent by the grand baroque fireplace in white and gold and the highly polished bookcases against the wall opposite the throne.

Once inside the room, all but two of the functionaries melted away and Spartov was left standing in the middle of the room with Peter Dunne. Temporarily, he was at a loss, then he remembered that he was, above all, the informal Pope.

'Will you use the throne, Holy Father?' asked Peter?'

'Who is first?'

'Angelo Rossetti, he has served for fifty years as sacristan at his local church in Palermo.' Peter was reading from his notes. 'Perhaps you may recall that you wished to present him personally with the Bene Merenti medal'

'Ah yes, lied Spartov. 'Just ask him to come in. You may leave us now,' addressed to two highly decorated chamberlains who hovered uncertainly at the door. They backed out of the door. Seconds later, the door opened again and Signor Rossetti was announced. He was a man of about eighty, white haired and wrinkled, He was dressed in his Sunday best and very erect. The occasion was clearly almost too much for him and, as he walked towards the Pope, tears ran down his parchment cheeks. Spartov walked to him with outstretched arms. 'Signor Rossetti, what a pleasure to meet you.' The old man stared fixedly at Spartov through rapidly blinking eyes. 'Holy Father I...it is...' He trailed off in confusion but already Spartov's arms were guiding him to one of the chairs, where he sat as though in shock while Spartov settled himself in a chair opposite. Peter positioned himself to Spartov's right and smiled encouragingly at Rossetti.

'Tell me about yourself,' said Spartov. 'Your wife, children, have you grandchildren?' The old man clicked out of his stupor and began to talk, slowly and hesitantly at first then, with increasing animation about his apparently inexhaustible supply of relatives. Spartov sat easily, smiling and nodding. After some ten minutes of conversation Peter coughed discreetly and handed Spartov a small white box surmounted by the Papal coat of arms. Taking the box, Spartov turned to Signor Rossetti and said: 'I was so interested in what you were saying that I quite forgot the real purpose of your visit. Fortunately, I have a two-legged conscience here who reminds me of these things. Perhaps we had better stand otherwise you will tell your family that the Pope did not present your medal properly.'

Rossetti suddenly recollected where he was and jerked to his feet ass if operated by strings.

'Take this with our Apostolic Blessing for you and your family. May the peace of Christ be with you always.' Spartov mentally vomited as he forced himself to say the words. Rossetti, oblivious of Spartov's mental turmoil dropped to an aged knee and grasped Spartov's hand between his own. 'Surely, surely, Holy Father. This has been the inspiring moment of my life.'

As Rossetti was shown out, leaking tears down his shirt front once again, Spartov ran a hand across his forehead. He felt exhausted already. One hour, two bishops, an author and two disabled children later, he wondered if he would be able to go on. The routine was almost standard. The visitor entered, shyly or with supreme self-confidence only to be struck dumb when actually face to face with whom they assumed to be the Pontiff. Spartov put each one at their ease, chatted then bid farewell with a few sacrilegious words about God and Peace.

'Let me rest for a moment, Monsignor.' Spartov sank into a chair. 'Are there many more?' 'Only one, Holy Father,' said Peter as he hurried to inform the chamberlain to wait for a few moments. He returned to the Pope, looking concerned. 'I know it is not my place but perhaps Your Holiness should reduce the numbers of people you see in private audience. I know you realize how much it means to them all, but it is very exhausting for you.'

'You can say that again,' thought Spartov, and this is only my first day. Perhaps it will get better. But, in truth, he was badly shaken by the effect he had on the people who came to see him. He had expected respect, but he was quite unprepared for what appeared to be genuine affection. His own actions and words revolted him. A revulsion he found difficult to put into definable terms. After all, he had trained for four years to be Celavsky. The difference between learning and doing was immense; he should have known that and been prepared for it. He was, or had been, a soldier. But the reality was far different from his imaginings. That was what was upsetting him. He must get completely under control. Now that he was Pope, he was in a position to give maximum effect to his objective. He roused himself with an effort, conscious that his young English private secretary was looking at him curiously. He would have to be very careful about Monsignor Dunne; he was a very bright priest.

You seem strangely depressed Holy Father.'

'Just a moment of tiredness. Don't look so worried. Who is next?'

'The Russian Ambassador, who expressly wished to meet you after your return from Czechoslovakia. Boris Puvinski is his name you will remember. I think you should be on your throne to receive him at least.'

'Yes of course,' walking to the dais. He knew little about the man, he would soon find out. He certainly worked quickly and that was a relief anyhow. 'I will see him alone.'

Peter shot a puzzled look and Spartov saw that he had phrased it badly. He tried to rectify the situation. 'He may feel better able to speak freely.' Peter nodded, but without any great conviction and Spartov cursed irreligious oath under his breath as Peter went to the door.

Puvinski was probably the largest man Spartov had ever seen not excluding Kutznov. He was built like an Olympic weightlifter. His diplomatic white and black suit bulged with layers of fat. A square head with close cropped white hair, slightly too small for the body, increased the sense of overall size if that was possible. He was about the same age as Spartov with features resembling the work of a particularly uninspired four-year-old child. 'Your Holiness,' he said stiffly bowing. 'Well Comrade Puvinski, we have succeeded.' Spartov's face broke into a grin. Puvinski relaxed.

'The likeness is remarkable, so remarkable that I had a moment's panic, when I saw you, that our plan had failed.' 'No, it has succeeded this far, splendidly.' Spartov had taken an instant dislike to Puvinski. Perhaps it was his manner or his swagger. No, it was something, which again, he could not put into words. Spartov sighed mentally. So many things had happened so quickly in the last few days that he was unable to think clearly yet.

Puvinski took his enormous weight off his enormous feet and sank down into one of the chairs. 'I am here, officially, to present my respects to you on your historic visit to your home country. In fact, I have to brief you on your main target. The gathering of cardinals and bishops which Leo announced is to take place next year. It will be your job to see that the Synod breaks up in dissension. In the space of two or three years, if you play your part well, comrade, the influence of the Church can be reduced considerably and the Papacy discredited. You have a golden opportunity during this Synod, of which everyone hopes so much. Do not fail to grasp it. Your contact for passing other items of interest is Franco Esseppi, a gardener employed here in the Vatican. He was introduced several years ago and you will have the opportunity to see him every day during your walks in the garden. He will also give you messages. It would not do for the Russian Ambassador to be a frequent visitor, eh?' Puvinski smiled to reveal a mouth full of gold. It looked obscene.

Spartov tried not to look at the Ambassador. 'How many people, here in Rome, know the truth?' Just myself and Esseppi. Although an Italian, he is completely trustworthy. He is the best kind of traitor, he is thoroughly stupid. 'By which statement Puvinski revealed not a little stupidity in his own character, which Spartov was quick to notice. He was taken aback by the other's attitude. He leaned forward and gripped the arms of the throne with white knuckles. Puvinski leered. 'There are a lot of stupid people around,' he said with unconscious irony. He began to laugh out loud, stopping suddenly with a bout of coughing and wheezing.

Spartov was glad when Puvinski left and Peter returned. After lunch in the cheerless dining room and a twenty-minute rest in an equally cheerless, but slightly more comfortable, sitting room next door, he signalled to a chamberlain and a few minutes later he was whisked down in the private lift to the papal garage. Sarto was waiting at the door of an ancient Rolls and Spartov had just settled when the five-minute journey up the ramp and into the Vatican gardens ended. He got out, clutching the breviary which he remembered to bring, and stood for a moment watching the Rolls purr its way back to the garage. He was at one of the highest spots in the gardens. Shadowy lanes of arched Ilexes led off in all directions. Pines and Laurels formed little groups and, through them all, he could see the magnificent dome of the basilica over the mass of crimson-topped Cannas. The wintry sun was still warm. A little way off, he could see the worn stonework which he knew must be the wall of Leo IV, which divided the informal private garden from the more characteristic Italian garden layout around the radio and railway stations. In the weeks, no years, to come he would take pleasure in exploring the whole layout. One never knew, it might come in useful sometime. From the first moment in the gardens, where the only noise was the chatter of the birds, he knew that it would become his favourite place. Somewhere he could walk and think. He had a lot of thinking to do. His mind was a confused jumble of conflicting impressions. He had imagined that he would simply have to play a part while retaining his innermost thoughts intact. It was not going to be so simple. His role as Pope had already given him much more to think about than he would have believed possible.

'Holy Father.' Spartov spun around startled to see a squat roly-poly man with black hair slightly grey at the temples. He had tiny spectacles and he was dressed in the walking out dress of an archbishop. Although the day was warm, he wore a full length red-lined black cloak. He beamed all over his face. Spartov feigned delight while wondering who the hell he was. His mind quickly ran through its card index of faces and descriptions until it clicked the correct photo into place.

'Archbishop, what a nice surprise. Am I to have your company during my walk?'

'If your Holiness does not mind. I was so sorry to be indisposed during your visit, but I am quite recovered now and I should be interested to hear your comments.' Carelli still beamed as he fell into step with Spartov along one of the shaded paths. Spartov's mind raced. This was the Cardinal Secretary of State and no one had told him that he was missing from the tour of Czechoslovakia. He would have to be careful. Obviously, his information was not entirely complete; still, Carelli did not seem to suspect anything. With every new meeting of the Pope's staff, Spartov's confidence increased. Both his face and his manner must be convincing. He thought about reporting the oversight regarding Carelli to the Russians back in Moscow via the gardener. That, of course, would spell trouble for Granky, he would not want that; best to leave things.

He sympathised with Carelli's recent illness, without having the faintest idea what it was and then they discussed the visit in general terms. He was glad that Carelli did not want any details. Indeed, he seemed not to notice anything amiss and Spartov realized that he would have been fully informed about the visit from detailed reports received from his private secretary. He must remember to ask Peter

Dunne for copies, so that he could brief himself. Carelli was chirping away unconcerned, waving his arms and swirling his cloak.

'We must get to work on the Synod. Fix the date, send letters of invitation.' He stopped and looked Spartov in the face with such intensity that the agent thought he must have detected some flaw there, the small amount of plastic surgery perhaps? Spartov clenched his fists in readiness. He knew that he was quite capable of felling the cardinal with a single blow, what he would do with the body was a matter which he could solve with the aid of the gardener. When at last Carelli spoke, it was such an anti-climax, Spartov had to restrain himself from laughing out loud.

'This will be a milestone in the history of the Church, you can rely on me to do all in my power to make it a success.'

'Thank you, Eminence.' Success was the last thing Spartov wished for the Synod. 'We shall need the prayers of the whole Church.'

11. ARTHUR GETS READY

Friday, 24 November 1978

Maurice could not remember who it was who had said that Trastevere was Rome's dustbin, but he did not think it was deserved. He had walked the direct way and crossed the Tiber by the Ponte Palatino, making his way through the maze of narrow streets to a spot not far from the church of Santa Maria. Unlike Rex, he was interested in history and architecture. He had a tourist's attitude to both He could see that the district was poor and probably very ancient, the narrow streets, tiny piazzas and deteriorating facades showed evidence of that. But the place was alive with people and the wintry sunshine gave the most unpromising corners a facelift.

He sat at a table outside a small trattoria. The blue and white umbrellas were folded no doubt to take advantage of, rather than protect against, the sunshine. He sipped a cup of coffee and, under the pretext of studying 'La Monde', he examined a building on the opposite side of the piazza. It was very much like its neighbours, three storeys high with a red pantile roof and flaking stucco. The interest lay in the fact that this was the house chosen by Lia as the 'safe house' for the kidnapping. A broad arch interrupted the façade at ground level. He saw that it was closed by a metal shutter with a smaller wicket door inset. The archway would be access for a car. There was probably a garage behind it. There was no other door in front so it was a certainty that pedestrian access to the house was also behind the green shutter. He noticed that one or two houses on the opposite side of the small open piazza had a similar arrangement. It looked very convenient and, finishing his coffee, he got up and continued his perambulations through the piazza with its tiny fountain and into the half light of the street beyond.

***

Some half a mile to the south of the agreeable little piazza, Arthur Brown stood in the light of a small garage and admired the shiny black Mercedes. The whole of the rear passenger compartment was shielded from view behind tinted glass.

'That will do admirably,' he said.

The curly-black haired Italian grunted and wiped his hands on a strip of cloth so oily that it was not clear whether he was taking grease off his hands or putting it on. Arthur tapped the number plates with the silver-topped stick which he affected on his sorties into Rome. He looked enquiringly at the greasy young man.

'Here.; The Italian was clearly a man of few words. He opened the driver's door and flicked a switch, silently, the number plates at the front of the car revolved to present a blank face. Arthur picked his way through the jumble of tools and half dismantled engines to the rear of the car and saw that the same thing had happened there.

That's fine.' He took out his wallet and produced some notes. 'That is what we agreed,' The Italian took the notes and stuffed them into his pocket. 'I will bring you the other set of number plates eventually.' Arthur was nothing if not careful. He passed over some more notes. 'That will pay for garaging for the next four months. You understand that I may want the car at a moment's notice. How can I get into here if you are not around?' The Italian produced a key from a hook o the wall. 'I cannot say when I will be here, but this key will open the doors at the front.' He seemed uninterested.

Arthur pocketed the key with satisfaction. The garage had been recommended to him by Lia, she was invaluable. It was discreet, it specialised in unusual specifications for cars and it was run by one man, whose clumsy appearance belied his varied skills. So far as Lia knew, he had no connections with any organisation which might prove difficult. The garage was actually one of five separate compartments, set under a neglected warehouse in a dirty side street. It was ideal for his purpose.

'Will it take long to fix the plates when I bring them?'

'No, just a few minutes.'

12. GOODBYE KUTZNOV

Sunday, 26th November 1978

The air conditioning was working again and Kutznov and his five companions sat in comparative comfort around the conference table.

'Dr Klein has completed his examination of the body and there is little of significance which could cause trouble.' Kutznov sweated copiously and shifted about in his chair. 'Tell us about anything significant.' Kutznov told them, he really had no choice. Shortly afterwards he was making his last journey, through the Linanka crematorium, hard on the heels of Gregor and Vladimir. The only real difference was that Kutznov produced rather more ash. The new commander of the Linanka Complex, much to his surprise, was Colonel Rostock. He knew better than to enquire after his predecessor whose heath, he was informed, had taken a turn for the worse.

Monday, 27th November 1978

Seventy-year-old Dr Fedor Uglev was taken from his home quite suddenly the following day. His Prague clinic was closed while several men, not unlike Gregor and Vladimir in general appearance, systematically examined his files. Two of them systematically examined Dr Uglev who, in consequence, suffered a fatal heart attack. The files in question were not to be found; a matter of no surprise because they had nestled in the private office of the Pope's personal physician, Enrico Formenti, to whom Dr Uglev had sent them, by personal courier, immediately following the election of Leo XIV.

Five bull-necked gentlemen at the KGB central office in Moscow were not amused at the failure to find the files. Dr Uglev's clinic and residence were ordered to be accidentally burnt to the ground. It was unfortunate that Mrs Uglev was having a relaxing bath with her secret lover in the residence at the time; Mrs Uglev and her lover certainly thought so. All Rostock could do now was wait and see and send an urgent message to Spartov.

13. PROBLEMS

Wednesday, 29th November 1978

The days had grown colder and Spartov was warmly wrapped in a long scarlet cloak over his white soutane. He looked towards the dome of St Peter's, golden in the waning sun. The whole garden had taken on the tinge of Autumn. Peace, if he stretched out his hand he would be able to touch it, nearly. A man could walk in these gardens and forget the tiresome world. He saw why it was a favourite place of the popes. It was important that he did not forget the world; he had a particular mission to achieve. The garden was a seducer he would have to resist.

He sensed a movement close by and the gardener rested his wheelbarrow. Before the man had first made contact, Spartov had speculated upon each gardener in turn. The contact could hardly be the young boy with spiky hair who scuttled away in fear at his approach. It could be either of the two weather-beaten men who were to be seen constantly tending the shrubberies, or the capable-looking man in overalls. In fact, the contact turned out to be a man of maybe sixty or so years with snow white hair and grave demeaner, whom he seldom saw doing anything.

Esseppi imparted his message in a few terse sentences.

'You're quite certain of this?' Spartov suddenly cold, not because of the temperature but deep, deep cold inside where it did not show. It was as if he had taken on every physical attribute of Celavsky.

'I am certain I got the message right. You are to do what you think best,' said Esseppi woodenly. He muttered something unintelligible under his breath and departed with his barrow. He would not go far, Spartov knew, just out of sight where he could sit and think about whatever elderly gardeners thought about.

Spartov continued with his walk. The message explained something that had been worrying him. Professor Formenti had been insistent upon giving him a thorough physical examination. He was glad he had deferred the matter. A complete physical examination could not be allowed in any case; Klein had been quite positive on the point. The minute scars left by the small amount of plastic surgery would be too apparent to a doctor's trained eye.

There seemed to be nothing but problems. He had not become used to his daily audiences as he had hoped and the information he received from all quarters of the world, the difficulties to be overcome, the sheer paperwork weighed heavily on him. He would be able to pass information to Moscow via the gardener but he did not quite get the satisfaction he had hope for. It had become clear that the trappings of luxury were reserved for his public image. His private quarters, meals and what was euphemistically termed his leisure were austere in the extreme. Peter had informed him enthusiastically that Paul VI had actually worn a hair shirt next to his skin, a habit Spartov was in no hurry to emulate. He was rapidly revising his opinion of the occupants of Peter's throne. Whatever their outward appearance, they all seemed to have been intensely dedicated men, though misguided of course. It explained a lot. How the Church had survived. He had read some of his predecessors' private notes. He told himself that he was hoping to find ammunition for his battle with the Synod, not admitting that he was looking for confirmation of his own position – an agent sworn to destroy the Church. The notes were all meditations of various kinds. He knew it was religious drivel, but he felt uneasy. He must get a grip on the situation and regain his earlier detachment. That very morning, he had caught himself sincerely trying to comfort a bereaved widow; and then there was the business of South America.

***

Arthur parked the little blue Fiat at the corner of the Via degli Annibaldi and glanced briefly at the Colosseum. It formed not quite a perfect cylinder from the place where he stood. Large portions of the arcaded walls had fallen away with the passage of centuries. Traffic swirled around the old gladiatorial battleground daring the tourists to try and make it there and back again. Arthur thought he would have faced the lions first. He turned his back on the scene and made his way to the telephone box where he carefully wrote down the number in a small notebook. He returned to his car and consulted his book. That was the fourth number. He looked at the next place on his schedule and marked it on the map spread out over the front seat. The railway station, damn, he had not sorted the locations properly. He felt annoyed with himself. He laid great stress on careful planning. He started the car and made a long detour to avoid the Colosseum.

***

Peter Dunne watched the water jumping and splashing around the bronze seventeenth century sailing ship, known as the galera, which sat in the middle of a small lake between the outer walls and those of the museum. It had been designed by the celebrated architect Carlo Maderno and Peter never tired of watching the fountains of water which spouted, when it was working, from the masts and gun barrels. He sat on the marble seat, a little chilly at that time of year, and worried. Peter was not naturally a worrying person but Leo was giving him some concern. It was natural that a new Pope should generate excitement and, as with everything new, there was what was known as the 'honeymoon period' which should not yet be over but, to some extent, it was.

When first elected, Leo had been dynamic and unpredictable but lately he had become rather less dynamic and more preoccupied. It seemed to date from his visit to Czechoslovakia. Possibly it had depressed him and it would pass. Still, it had caused him to make one or two slips. The speech he gave before the assembly of Rome's parish priests for example, the week before. If Peter had not taken care to check the Pope's draft sermon minutely, he might have missed what the Pope had evidently missed himself. Certain parts of the speech could be taken almost as a papal endorsement of communism. Fortunately, there had been time to clarify the wording and have it retyped for the meeting, Leo had not been very pleased at the alterations until the full import had been explained to him and then he calmed down. It was the first time Peter had seen Leo really angry. There had been a few similar instances when his replies to foreign statesmen had required amendment. It was almost as though the Pope suffered bouts of mental confusion from time to time; but he was perfectly lucid and correct in normal conversation.

'May I join you in a state of spiritual ecstasy?'

Peter came out of his reverie with a jolt to find an aged priest had been standing watching him, hands tucked into the sleeves of his soutane against the chill. Peter had seen him in the curial offices, sitting at a desk even more decrepit than he was, but he was not quite sure of his precise function. His face was lined, his head almost completely bald.

'No, I am hardly in a state of spiritual ecstasy. I am just letting my thoughts wander. Join me by all means, but you will think it a very idle pastime.' 'Not at all,' replied the old man, taking a seat on the cold marble. 'You have a very responsible position. You must let your mind go into neutral, in a manner of speaking, otherwise it will seize up. His Holiness is a hard taskmaster I imagine?' 'He is, but I realize that I am uniquely privileged to serve him.' Peter was apt to be overtaken by bouts of humility.

'What were you looking so worried about?' The old man's eyes regarded Peter with a kindly, if rheumy, gaze. 'Can I help you?'

'I was merely speculating.'

'What about?'

'What would happen if the Pope went mad, I mean really insane, not violent, but unable to properly carry out his duties?' Peter stopped abruptly, wondering if he had said too much. 'There would be some who would say that nobody would know the difference.' The old man sat with his hands on his knees, head sunk into his shoulders like some benevolent bird of prey. Peter noticed that his cassock was almost as old as its inhabitant. 'Seriously, I can't remember such a thing ever happening, although there have certainly been some odd popes in history. I suppose the College of Cardinals would have to take some action. Quiet removal to a monastery and a new election; what a fine scandal that would make eh? Thank goodness we don't have to do any speculating about the present Holy Father, he's really brought a breath of sanity to the Church. I don't expect to see his successor.'

Peter hoped the old man was right, but his doubts still persisted. The talk drifted to other things, the weather, the influence of the communists among the grass roots of the Church and the Pope's visit to South America.

14. LIA HAS FUN

Wednesday, 29th November 1978.

Lia Ortello wondered if she would manage to contain herself. She sat toying with a drink and glancing through the glossy magazine on her lap. She had already bought everything in it ten times over in her mind. Why did everything take so long? The idea that had been forming in her mind suddenly crystallised and she picked up the telephone and dialled a number.

'Room 64,' she said. There was a pause while the connection was made then:

'Hello, who the hell is that?' Rex sounded as though he had just woken up, which in fact, he had.

'Lia, and don't be so grumpy. It's nine o'clock at night. Don't say you just got up!' There was a hint of malice in her voice. Rex was alert immediately.

'I had a heavy night. Not much else to do in this God-forsaken dump.' No one but Rex Carter could have seriously held such a view nor picked such an unhappy combination of words to describe it. But Rex was a weird character, which was part of his fascination, to certain people at least.

'I'm at a loose end too tonight, Rex. Why don't you come over and keep me company? I have some wine and I'm sure we can think of something to pass the time.' The slightly husky quality in her voice and the promise of an interesting evening quickly decided Rex that it was playtime.

'Where are you now? I'll be right over.'

Lia gave the necessary directions and replaced the receiver with a smile. She felt pleased with herself. She had no reason to doubt that Arthur Brown's scheme would be successful. He had too much of the quiet purposeful air of the true fanatic to fail. In her experience, it was not failure which caused problems, but the aftermath of success. She knew that, however big the rewards, greed would enter the arena like a hungry lion. It would be good to have someone she could rely on. She had no doubts about her ability to seduce Rex. No seduction was necessary in his case. More importantly, she knew that, with her experience, she could keep him interested, not to say snared, for as long as she cared.

Arthur had given the others some indication of her early history when he said that she had been a prostitute in Naples. What he had not said was that she had very little choice in the matter. She had been the result of a casual liaison between her mother, from whom she had inherited her startling good looks, and an unknown English soldier. When asked what her father did, she usually said that he had died fighting for his country. He had been blown up by a land mine a few days after he had left her mother, but he had not been fighting for her country.

From her teenage discovery that she had no difficulty attracting men, she managed to keep herself in reasonable comfort. The life was precarious in more ways than one and she regularly found herself in awkward situations; particularly with clients who felt no urgency to settle their debts in cash. More that once she had dragged herself home, torn and bloodied by drunken fists. After one such incident, when she was prevented from plying her profession for more than a week by a badly swollen lip, she was taken on one side by her mother. 'Lia I would not have chosen this way of life for you. I had hoped for something better; but I am in no position to offer reproaches. I can offer this.' She gave her a long steel hatpin and spent some time instructing her in its use.

Ironically, she found no cause to use it for several months. Her clients, drawn from the docks, the taverns and occasionally the better off in fast cars, gave her no trouble. Then came the night she would not forget. The man was big and muscular. He had agreed her fee without any attempt to barter. The place was the back of his truck. After she had performed her side of the bargain, he was in no mood to part with his lire. 'Here, this is what I think of you,' he muttered. It was dark. She was sitting with her back against the side of the truck, he was kneeling over her. He aimed a giant fist at her head. She ducked and he missed, swaying around drunkenly. She drew the hat pin and used it in an underarm jab of fearful accuracy. He froze with the sickening pain and clutched between his legs with both hands. Blood started to drip through his fingers. He had lost all interest in her and in any other woman for some time to come. She had all the time in the world to extract all the money from his wallet, gather her coat, arrange her dress and run from the truck. She glanced back as she was leaving to see that he had toppled over and he was rolling on the floor, moaning in agony.

She felt nauseated but pleased with herself. He would have cared little if she had left with a bloody nose or worse. From that moment she knew that she would never be at the mercy of any man again.

Lia had ambition and brief encounters in the back seats of parked cars for a few hundred lira a time soon seemed very small reward. When she was twenty-five she arrived in Rome and gravitated, quite naturally to the Via Vittorio Venito. She owed her modest success to a chance meeting with Giancallo Geneti, apparently a businessman, whom she encountered outside one of the smart cafés. He wanted her and she had no feelings about the matter at first, so long as the money was right. He whisked her off to his villa outside Rome in the Alban Hills.

For ten years she functioned, first as his mistress, gradually as his confidant. Geneti, she discovered, was a relatively minor Mafiosa boss, kind to her but ruthless with others. His modest empire embraced several respectable hotels and a highly select brothel, situated in a tangle of streets behind the church of San Trinita dei Monte, over which he installed her in a luxurious apartment.

Her association with Geneti had ended somewhat abruptly when he was found discharging his lungs in a bloody mess all over the pavement in the Piazza di Spagna. He had been given a lead coated emetic by a rival. His funeral was sumptuous and neat to make amends for the uncharacteristically untidy manner of his demise.

Lia found herself without a friend. She had a genuine affection for the coarse Mafia chief and shed real tears at his funeral. More importantly, she was without the money she loved only a little more than Geneti himself. He did not leave her totally destitute. The select brothel and apartment were hers but there was not a lot of cash to spare for her, by now expensive tastes. She could have made more immediately, for the brothel was noted for being discreet and only she knew the names of the very many diplomats, actors and prelates who made use of its facilities. Several highly placed politicians were on her books and, had she turned to blackmail, she would, no doubt, have made a steady and not inconsiderable income. Although she had pondered the idea, it was self-defeating. The brothel owed its success to the fact that its clients could be sure of absolute secrecy. Take that away and the word would soon spread. Also, blackmailers were notoriously short-lived and Lia enjoyed life. So, she turned to expanding her business in other, less salubrious quarters of the city, but it was not the way to a fortune and Lia badly needed a fortune. She needed money like an addict needs a fix. The sight of money in bulk was enough to give her an orgasm. Hence, her willingness to join Arthur in his plan to secure limitless wealth. Her years with Geneti had taught her caution, however, and Rex would be her insurance policy.

Her apartment had a private entrance and she welcomed Rex warmly when he arrived. He had not bothered to dress up. An old windcheater covered open necked shirt and jeans. He said little and his eyes were cold, but by morning he envied not one of the clients of the fine little whores busy on the floor below, and they knew their jobs.

He turned over in bed as the cold morning light crept around the heavy curtains. 'What kind of place do you run here?'

She lay naked under the single sheet, damp with their nocturnal exertions. 'It's better if you don't know. Aren't you satisfied?' In answer, he reached for her again and slippery wet flesh joined together once more. As he lay back twitching, she said, 'Would you like to do this more often?' The look in his pale blue eyes told her all she wanted to know.

She had paid the premium, the first of many, and the policy was in force. She would be almost sorry when it matured.

15. MORE PROBLEMS

Thursday, 30th November 1978

'I hope that our visit to South America will bring some relief to that miserable continent.' Peter shuffled some papers on his knee. 'I'm sure the clergy and people will be greatly strengthened.'

Spartov consulted his diary. 'We are due to arrive on Monday, 18th December. The regime is Fascist and oppressive and I shall do all in my power to support the poor in their struggle, Monsignor.' He looked upon the visit as a golden opportunity to add fuel to the unrest already present. He would have to be careful but, if the people could be persuaded to revolt, the result would almost certainly be another communist state.

The air in the papal study was heavy with cigarette smoke as the two men went over the tight schedule of the forthcoming visit. After a further hour of talking, Peter indicated that the time had come to meet a group of pilgrims from Czechoslovakia.

The applause from the assembled group of pilgrims was rapturous. There were about two hundred of them in the large audience room. Spartov moved among them smiling and laughing. Children's tousled heads were treated to the papal rub and broad labourers' backs were slapped vigorously. Papal functionaries were at a minimum.

The crowd parted at one point and a broad-shouldered, middle-aged man of about Spartov's height stepped forward with arms outstretched. A broad grin adorned his face and he clasped Spartov by the shoulders. Standing at one side of the room, Cardinal Carelli, smiled broadly at the reunion he had so carefully and secretly arranged.

'Wenceslas!'

Spartov would have stepped back but he was clasped too firmly. He fixed a grin on his face as he desperately searched his memory in vain for some clue to the face in front of him. This time the mental file did not oblige. Clearly, the man knew him, clearly, he knew him well. He did the only thing he could do and moved forward to clasp the man in warm embrace.

'What a surprise. Who is responsible?' Spartov looked at Carelli.

'I thought Your Holiness would enjoy meeting your old friend from the hill-walking centre at Brno.'

'You did well, Eminence.' He turned to the grinning Czech, grasping at the clue. 'How I wish we could have time to talk over old days, you have not changed a bit since we trekked over the hills together. Fortunately, the Pope belongs to everyone but himself.' Spartov hurriedly passed on, smile still pasted on his face, inwardly fuming that the Celavsky dossier had let him down once again. He thought that Kutznov should be shot, unaware that his wish had been anticipated and the stout colonel was already being recycled. He was pleased, however, that he had carried off the occasion so well. It could have been a disaster. He sweated, although the day was not warm.

Peter Dunne, to say nothing of the broad-shouldered man now lost in the crush, was less happy. Leo obviously had a slip of memory. The Czech had never walked in the hills with Celavsky. He had been a cook at the centre and shared many convivial evenings with Celavsky, both at the centre and at the episcopal residence in Prague. Clearly Leo had mistaken him for someone else thought Peter. Carelli thought he understood.

Spartov had difficulty extracting himself from the forest of arms reaching out to touch him and he was relieved when he was retracing his steps to his study, Peter in attendance.

Professor Formenti was awaiting him when they arrived at the study and Spartov told Peter that he could go. Formenti wasted no time, 'Holy Father, I must insist that you have a proper medical examination without delay.' Spartov had settled himself behind the desk. Formenti settled himself in front; as welcome as a match in a firework factory. Spartov had decided on his tactics.

'Why do you distress yourself, Professor?'

'Holy Father, you recall that, a week after your election, I received your medical files from your personal physician in Prague. I immediately gave you an examination and confirmed, as far as possible, Dr Uglev's diagnosis. Had it not been for the election you would have already had the operation to remove the growth. At the moment, your cancer is in its primary stages, the ideal time to operate. I suggest that you have immediate further tests and an operation to remove the growth. You must cancel your trip to South America or I cannot be responsible for the consequences.'

Spartov leaned forward and spread his hands on the desk. 'And how long will all this take? How long that is before I can fully resume my duties?' Formenti looked troubled. 'Well, if all goes well, light duties in say three months, possibly a further three months before you take up full duties again.'

'Then, dear Professor, the whole thing is out of the question.' Spartov smiled serenely. Formenti stared helplessly, having fallen into the trap.

'But, Holy Father ...'

'Professor, Christ's Vicar on Earth cannot simply take the next six months off. Consider, my illustrious predecessor reigned for little more than a month. What will the world think if it is announced that I am stricken with a possibly mortal illness? My duty is clear. I will put my trust in God and he will sustain me. Do you not believe in miracles?' Spartov, who most definitely did not believe in miracles nor any of the other nonsense which he had to say was struck by the irony of the situation when, by putting the nonsense into words he could extract himself from a tight corner.

Formenti removed his spectacles and commenced polishing the spotlessly clean lenses on an equally spotless handkerchief. His movements betrayed his extreme agitation. 'I do not know what to say.'

'Then say nothing and accept the will of God as we do.' Spartov had purposely lapsed into the sovereign 'we' to stress his position, a fact which did not escape Formenti. In the old days Spartov would have called it pulling rank. 'After all, where would we be if the Almighty turned away His attention for six seconds not six months? We would be nothing. There is no possibility that we can undertake the operative procedure you suggest and still continue to govern Christ's Church, a sacred obligation entrusted to us by Christ himself. If He calls, we are ready. If it pleases Him to prolong our earthly term until we have accomplished that which we set out to do, we will give thanks. We are appreciative of your concern, dear Professor, and you have our paternal and Apostolic Blessing.'

Spartov was quite enjoying himself, the more so as he saw the conflicting emotions, professional and pious, which chased themselves across the doctor's lined face.

'If you have quite made up your mind?' Formenti replaced his spectacles.

'We have.'

'I must depart and offer, in lieu of my professional expertise, my sincere prayers.'

'What more can we ask?'

Formenti departed while Spartov laughed silently to himself.

16. ARTHUR'S SAFE HOUSE

Friday, 1 December 1978.

Maurice rang the bell next to the metal shutter. He wore a heavy overcoat against the cold.

'Who is it'

'Maurice.' He felt conspicuous, although it was dark and there were few people about. A wave of singing drifted across from the brightly lit windows of the trattoria. Footsteps sounded behind the metal shutter. The footsteps stopped. Clunk, clunk, clunk and the shutter started to rise. It continued rising, now smoothly and silently in the newly greased steel guides. Maurice waited until it was level with his eyes, then ducked under and moved quickly into the dark interior. The shutter dropped rapidly and, as the bottom connected with the socket in the floor, the light was switched on. Arthur bent down and attended to the lock as Maurice looked about him. They were standing in a garage about five metres wide, running the depth of the building. A shutter, similar to the one at the front, closed off the other end. An unshaded light bulb glittered tactlessly from the ceiling. Flakes of plaster hung off the walls. The garage was completely empty except for a small blue Fiat.

'Come on up.' Arthur waved Maurice to a small door to his left. He had not noticed it before. It was painted the same pale green as the rest of the garage. They ascended a flight of stone steps to a single door at the top. They stepped through and Maurice found himself in a large room, comfortably furnished with armchairs and rugs. Heavy curtains covered the windows, from a record-player against one wall came the faint strains of a tenor struggling despairingly with an unidentified piece of Italian opera. Rex and Lia, sitting on cushions on the floor, moved slightly as though interrupted during a shared confidence. Rex stared at Maurice blankly, Lia gave him a slight smile, her hand resting possessively on Rex's arm. Maurice returned the smile with as much sincerity as he could muster. He found it difficult to like Lia. She was outstandingly attractive but, ever since that evening in London, how many months had it been? He never saw her without a mental picture. In it she was drooling over a stack of dollar bills.

Arthur was bustling about at a cabinet in the corner, every inch the genial host. Maurice thought he really would sell them some insurance before the night was out. What an incredible man. His face was flushed, whether with excitement, the heat or just a little over-indulgence in wine, it was hard to decide. Unlikely to be wine, Arthur was almost puritan in some ways. That was it, he had obviously missed his vocation; he should have been a monk! While Maurice amused himself with idle speculation, Arthur finished at the cabinet.

'You will have some wine, Maurice?' Arthur handed him a glass. 'Sit down, sit down do.' Maurice complied. Arthur settled himself in the chair opposite. Lia drew her knees up under her chin and clasped her bare legs beneath the hem of her skirt. Arthur sipped his drink appreciatively. 'I think I could get used to living in Rome, so sad to think that none of us will be able to come back afterwards. Enough of that, what do you think of this place?' 'It seems alright from what I have seen of it, which isn't much.' Maurice glanced around the room.

'Well, of course, you haven't seen the half of it yet. None of you have but let's go on a guided tour, shall we?' Arthur stood up and the others followed suit. 'Through here is a corridor leading to a bathroom, kitchen and two bedrooms. The kitchen is well equipped and I am gradually stocking the freezer so that we will have provisions for a long wait if necessary.'

They inspected the rooms.

'There are only two bedrooms and there are four of us, to say nothing of our hostage,' said Lia. 'Ah' Arthur chuckled like a small boy displaying his latest toy. 'Two of us can use the bedrooms and the other two can sleep in the living room. It is quite comfortable, plenty of cushions. It should not be for long. I estimate a week or two at the outside. As for our hostage.' He opened another door opposite the last bedroom from which a flight of wooden steps ascended. 'These will be his quarters.' He switched on the light and led the way up the narrow stairs. At the top he unlocked a door. They followed him through and found themselves in a large room which evidently covered most of the floor area of the house. It was thickly carpeted and there was a bed against the wall. Only one wall, opposite the bed, sported any windows and they were covered with wooden shutters secured with shiny new brass padlocks. 'There is a small bathroom at the end through that door, nothing else.'

Rex went over and assured himself that the bathroom led nowhere. 'Good,' he said. 'But a determined man might break through the shutters or call for help.' It was a long speech for Rex. Arthur walked over to the bed and, from under the top sheet he took a long steel chain. At one end was a thick bracelet, the other was secured to a solid-looking ring embedded in the wall. 'The length is sufficient to enable our hostage to reach the bathroom and the bed, but not the door or the windows. The shutters have been lined with felt and fit tightly to make the room completely soundproof. The walls are nearly two feet thick. I have checked' Maurice could well imagine that he had. 'Moreover, one of us will stay here with him during the whole time. We will arrange it in shifts.'

They descended the stairs again and settled back into their places. Arthur poured more wine.

'I expect the snatch to take place in about two months' time, at the end of the Synod.' He smiled. 'No, it's not out of any consideration for the Synod. It just happens to be the most propitious time.'

'I don't see...' began Rex.

'Let me explain. The whole point about the Pope is what I might call his unpredictable predictability, or vice versa if you prefer. While you two.' He waved a beautifully manicured hand at Rex and Maurice. 'While you have been acquainting yourselves with the back streets of Rome and Lia has been getting on with her illegal business, I have been studying the papal routine. Oh yes, there is a routine. I have carefully studied the times the Pope informally comes out of the Vatican. Most of the information is published in the press, after the event of course. Usually, he dresses as a simple priest, all in black. He has with him only the chauffer and his private secretary. Maurice, your friendship with Sarto has been invaluable here.' Arthur turned a beaming smile upon Maurice, who felt a little sick at the podgy cheeks and wet lips. 'He visits prisons, hospitals, schools but especially sick clergy. That's why the Synod is such a God-send, if I may use the phrase.'

Lia and Maurice looked blank. Rex seemed to be about to start slashing the cushions in boredom. How would he cope with being confined to the house after the kidnap, it was hard to judge? 'Get to the point,

Arthur,' he said. Arthur gave him a long refrigerating look and deliberately turned his attention to Maurice.

'One of the bishops, who is in Rome for the Synod, is a very old friend of the Pope from Czechoslovakia – Bishop Horniev. He is old in both senses of the word. They have been friends for about forty years and the Bishop is about seventy. The Pope was his protégé.'

'But surely he cannot be bribed?' Lia was still puzzled but interested. Arthur, sensing her interest, became enthusiastic.

'There is no question of bribery, it would be foolish to try. During the Synod, he is staying at the Venerable English College in Rome where the rector is another friend of his. Bishop Horniev has suffered from a mild heart disorder for a number of years. The Pope will naturally be upset when his old friend is stricken with what could be a serious heart attack at the end of the Synod. I am sure he will come rushing to his side.'

The dawn of understanding painted the faces of Lia and Maurice. Rex, for whom nothing subtler than a bloodstained knife had any meaning, continued to eye the cushions in unfriendly fashion. Arthur looked pleased with himself.

'I think that's all you need to know for the moment. Before you go, however, we must agree a timetable.' Arthur took out his notebook and consulted one of the pages. 'Lia, you must let everyone in your immediate circle know that you are going to Naples to visit your mother. Go by taxi to the station two weeks from today and by a ticket for the one-thirty Rapido. I will pick you up from there at one-thirty-five. Rex, you must leave your hotel three days later, make a reservation on the way to Milan and make your way here. The following day, Maurice, you must make sure to let your friend Sarto know that you are leaving for Paris for a short holiday. You, too, make your way here. The Synod is due to end, as I said, in two months. The day following the end of the Synod will be crucial.'

17. MOSCOW IS IMPATIENT

Sunday, 3 December 1978.

The five bull-necks were concerned. It showed in the way that none of them smoked during the brief meeting. 'Spartov has missed several opportunities.'

'Perhaps we should give him time. His reports have been most illuminating.'

'There is that of course but his speeches could be a little more inventive. He should not overdo the effort to imitate Leo.'

Elderly bull-neck five was impatient to get away for the weekend to his private dacha where good food, fine wines and a well-endowed red-haired girl were awaiting his attention. 'The meeting of cardinals and bishops is scheduled to take place in the new year. He should be preparing the ground with some infiltration of his speeches with socialist philosophy. I propose that we send a message to that effect at once.' They were all tired and so it was agreed. The coming Synod, after all, was of the utmost importance. If Spartov could cause its failure that could be a prelude to the collapse of the Roman Catholic Church as a whole.

Thursday, 7 December 1978

'Tell them there are difficulties. I am not such a free agent as we thought.' Spartov was angry.

Ambassador Puvinski remained unimpressed. 'It is not easy, Comrade, to invent a plausible excuse to see you and Moscow is waiting to see some results. I know you have been in this position for only weeks, but long enough to deliver some important speeches. You do not appear to have taken advantage of the situation.' Puvinski's square face was shiny with sweat as he shifted his position in the chair. The legs creaked in anguish as his enormous bulk moved.

'You forget yourself, Ambassador.'

'No, you forget yourself, Comrade. You were sent here for a purpose – to destroy the Roman Catholic Church from within. You are uniquely placed for that.'

Spartov stood up from his throne, aware that he was visibly trembling with anger at the odious character of a man sprawled in front of him, but unable to control himself. He was not altogether sure why he should be angry. It was not just the annoyance of someone who had been rebuked for failing to do his job properly, after all he was in Rome to do the bidding of his government. He slowly realized, long after Puvinski had gone, that he was angry that the Ambassador had spoken like that to the Pope. He must be very careful. The cogwheels of the dual personality were beginning to mesh together too freely and with too little effort. He would have to pull himself together when he got to South America,

18. SEEDS

Wednesday, 13 December 1978

The old gardener should have retired years ago. Esseppi was nearer seventy than sixty. His usefulness in the Vatican gardens was minimal. A spot of pruning and collecting dry leaves was a heavy day, but his principal function appeared to consist of sitting in a wheelbarrow, smoking a blackened pipe. He had worked or sat in the gardens for more than forty years and the official under whose jurisdiction he came had never thought of suggesting retirement. The official in question, who nursed an abiding hatred of all growing things, never saw the gardeners at all and seldom thought about them, unless one died or left and had to be replaced. So, Esseppi was allowed to potter on, ignored by his superiors, who scarcely knew of his existence, and humoured by his colleagues, to whom he rendered virtually no assistance.

His intelligence, as Puvinski had noted, was as limited as his physical capabilities. Thirty years before, the Russians had bought his services with a couple of bottles of red wine and a night at the local whorehouse. He was given modest payments when he delivered messages. He lived in the Vatican and never married. Indeed, he was the most saturnine man in the whole of the Vatican State and that was no mean achievement. He spoke, when he spoke at all, about shrubs and flowers. Surprisingly, he knew a great deal about them although he rarely proffered any advice on the subject. Indeed, he seemed to derive enormous satisfaction from not giving advice even, or perhaps especially, when asked.

Twice a week he tottered out of the Porta di Sant Anna into Rome itself. On Sundays he visited a trattoria not too far away, where he sat alone at a table in the corner drinking a bottle of wine until the morning Masses were over. Wednesdays, he ventured a little further afield to a local seed merchant, where he spent an hour or so propped against the counter engaged in gentle conversation with the proprietor or watching the customers come and go. The proprietor was virtually his only human contact. After his little outing, he would return to his wheelbarrow to rest and get over the excitement. He walked with a stick which he used to support himself and beat stray cats if any ventured near enough.

He was useful to the Russians, not because he was stupid, he did not know he was stupid, but because he was totally inconspicuous, a chameleon. They would have liked to have a much younger man inside the Vatican but, including Spartov, it was easier said than done.

The arrangements for delivery of messages was complicated but, as far as Esseppi was concerned, it simply involved him in passing a seed packet containing the message to the proprietor of the seed emporium. The message then went quickly, but by a circuitous route, to the Russian Embassy. The system had worked faultlessly for years, although it was only during the last few weeks that anything of real importance had been passed. It was pure chance, or some would say Divine intervention, that Pietro Thomaso, of the Departmento di Pubblica Sicurezza (Department of Public Security, a kind of Italian MI5) himself a rather dozy young man and totally ill-fitted for his job, called at the seed shop shortly after the gardener had deposited his seed packet. The shop happened to be crowded at that particular time, the proprietor was flustered and later in the day, the Russian Ambassador found himself the recipient of a small packet of Azealia seeds, while Thomaso, by now kitted out in shirt sleeves and old trousers, discovered that the third packet of seeds that he opened contained not seeds but a message. The message itself was fairly simple. It contained details of the American Ambassador's attitude to Church aid to Uganda. Dozy as he was, Thomaso could take the hint when it was handed to him on a plate, or in this case, a seed packet. He was out of his garden shed and at the desk of his superior officer as quickly as his third-hand scooter could take him.

His superior was Renaldo Mangini. Being not at all dozy, he realised that blessed fate had sent him a lead to probable espionage and almost certain promotion.

With a wife, mother and five children to support, he could do with a little promotion. He wasted no time in putting a watch on the seed merchant to await the next visit of the old gardener, for the manner of the discovery suggested him as the prime suspect. However, since the matter clearly concerned the Vatican, he would have to be careful.

The Russian Ambassador was not nearly as precipitate as the Italians. He knew that if he had received the seeds, someone else must have got the message. He sweated as he thought about it. With luck, whoever had bought the packet containing the message would return it to the shop, not understanding its significance. Without luck, the message might find its way to the police. There was no way the intricate network of contacts could be traced back to him but Moscow would not be pleased.

He mopped his forehead with a large silk handkerchief. The seed merchant was incompetent and he would have to be replaced as soon as he could arrange it. In the meantime, there was the matters of the message that Moscow would be expecting. With a certain degree of malice, Puvinski decided to inform Moscow that there had been no message from Spartov. A note to that effect was suitably encoded and transmitted to Moscow in the next diplomatic bag. It served to reinforce KGB fears about Spartov's progress and motives.

Saturday, 16 December 1978.

Lia was bored. She had bought her ticket, told her staff that she was going to Naples for a holiday, taken a taxi and been picked up by Arthur, all as arranged. She had wondered if there had been any special motive behind the fact that Arthur had singled her out to arrive first. She did not really think that Arthur had any designs on her virtue. That was a laugh in itself. Her virtue was long gone and she had formed the same conclusion as Maurice about Arthur's sexual inclinations – always assuming he had any.

She sat in the large living room and fiddled with a cup of coffee. Arthur had gone out again on some errand of his own. The occasional sound of a car drifted up from the square outside. She walked over and looked out of the window, keeping well back as Arthur had instructed her. Across the square was the small trattoria with the tables set out under a large striped awning. It was too cold for anyone to sit there, but the inside seemed to be well patronised with underemployed youths and old men, of which Italy seemed to have an inexhaustible supply. Squads of overfed Italian matrons, like huge black ants, bustled about among the shops which faced the trattoria across the tiny piazza. Someone had turned off the little Baroque fountain in the middle. The scene had a forlorn look about it. It was not so much waiting, as begging, for something to happen.

Lia turned away from the window. She had no need to explore the apartment. She had recommended it to Arthur in the first place because she knew it well. It had belonged to an important member of her deceased lover's staff. She had been there many times with Giancallo Geneti in the good days. It held many happy memories of pleasant evenings devoted to wine and song. It also held something else which she had judged prudent not to reveal to Arthur. A secondary means of escape. Some Italian apartments were not renowned for their fire escape provisions and there was nothing in the single access apartment to excite curiosity. Arthur's absence provided the opportunity to check that the escape route was still functioning properly.

She walked through into the narrow corridor and on, past the doors to the kitchen and bedrooms, to the end of the corridor next to the door leading to the upper staircase. The end of the corridor was rather extravagantly panelled in wood. She felt under one of the mouldings, trying to remember the exact spot to press. She found it after a bit of experimentation and she was rewarded with a faint click. She pulled on the moulding and the whole panel swung back to reveal that it was, in fact, a cunningly disguised door. A flight of steps led down through the darkness to where she knew there was another door at the bottom. She hesitated for a moment and then hurried down the steps. It was very cold and her scalp prickled with a tinge of anxiety.

She reached the bottom of the steps and felt for the door in the gloom. It had a modern spring-loaded bolt and she fumbled at the catch. To her relief, it actually moved easily and she was able to open the door and look out of the rear of the building past a tumble of huts crowded into the courtyard. It was completely enclosed except for a small archway almost directly opposite. Good, the route was still clear.

Arthur let himself in quietly. He crossed the living room and carefully opened the door to the corridor. He was in time to see Lia's back disappearing down the stairs. He closed the door again, smiling to himself. He had not survived for twenty-odd years in his line of business without taking careful precautions. He suspected everyone and trusted no one. It usually paid dividends. He let himself out of the door of the apartment and waited five minutes before letting himself in again. Lia was just coming into the living room.

'You're soon back,' she said.

'A short absence, but very profitable,' said Arthur, and meant it.

19. SOUTH AMERICA

Monday, 18 December 1978.

El Presidente Miguel Uvantes stood, wheezing slightly, in the middle of the tarmac, his narrow chest encased in medals, a high peaked cap surmounting his prune-like visage.

'What time does he arrive?'

One of the twenty heavily built bodyguards confirmed that the Pope was a few minutes overdue. The sun glinted on the line of sleek black limousines parked across the front of the welcoming dais. A considerable distance away, the airport buildings shimmered slightly in the haze. It was just possible to make out the multitudes of people jamming all vantage points. Every member of the ruling cabinet was standing on the dais and the President could not get out of his mind that a single bomb would remove the entire government with very little fuss. He had already ordered three searches of the dais and was contemplating a fourth when the Minister for State Security spotted the papal plane in the distance. The President threw a nervous glance at the Archbishop, who had been released from house arrest for the occasion and mopped his brow. He was head of the military junta which had seized power, by popular demand and armed force three years before. By all the yardsticks of South American politics, time was running out and he was conscious that his Swiss bank account was still far short of his target.

The huge white plane taxied up to the dais, steps were adjusted, the door opened and the Pope appeared to the sound of the city band, especially augmented for the occasion. Troops presented arms and guns fired a salute into the hot blue sky. Almost certainly, the crowds at the airport went wild with delight, but they could not be heard from the dais.

Spartov had brought with him a very small entourage consisting of Peter Dunne, Cardinal Carelli and the Vatican Press Officer. The last was a poker-faced individual whose main function was to give the Press as little information as possible. He carried out his duties with joyless efficiency, his releases giving no more insight than could have been obtained by staying at home and watching events on television.

Platitudinous speeches were exchanged and the President, with obvious relief, led the way to the official cavalcade. Expensive engines thrummed and the line of cars, now joined by scores of police outriders, glided slowly out of the airport, past the cheering crowds and onto the miles long road which led, straight as a die to the capital city. Armed troops lined the route and the lampposts were linked with white and gold streamers. The procession picked up speed and Spartov was spared the need to make small talk with the odious little President by returning the waves of the crowds who got no more than a glimpse of white as the cars sped past.

During the first day, the Pope was given a conducted tour of the State University, the lavish new concrete and glass hospital and the recently opened motor car factory. The routine was the same at each stop. The official motorcade drove up to the entrance. The crowds were held back at some distance by police. TV, Radio and Press were accommodated in a special stand to one side. A carefully rehearsed child presented a spray of flowers to the Pontiff, said child was then patted on the head by the president in full view of the Press before the party proceeded to make the tour. On the way out of the hospital, Spartov headed straight for the crowds, to their delight and the President's dismay. After several minutes of hand kissing, frenzied cheering and near hysterics on the part of some of the older ladies, Spartov was persuaded to return to the official car to be rushed off to his next assignment. The visits were interspersed with State banquets with chandeliers and gold plate. The guests seemed to be entirely generals and admirals.

***

On the morning of the second day, the itinerary was brought to Spartov's room after Mass at the Apostolic

Nunciature by Peter Dunne. Spartov looked at it briefly and decided the time had come to rebel.

'More factories, more visits to specially cleaned up cathedrals and sanitised flats in carefully laid out estates and carefully chosen tenants. No, absolutely no. I particularly asked to see the poor in their villages, God knows there are enough of them. We know they don't all live in modern blocks of flats. I must speak to the people. I have not been near them, simply whisked through crowds in a bullet-proof limousine. I don't want to meet generals and presidents. Ninety-nine per cent of the population are Catholic and about three-quarters live in squalor. Monsignor Dunne, summon me the man who is in charge of these visits. I want some changes made.'

General Xerces Caracco, a fat little man bustled pompously into the room some minutes later. He was desperately sorry but security precautions were strict. His Holiness would understand that, perhaps one or two selected people could be brought to the Holy Father but visits such as were being suggested would undermine the whole of the enlightened government's long-term proposals for improvement and reform, which he personally could assure the Holy Father were being strenuously pursued. The General spread his hands, palms down, to indicate the utter futility of pressing his demands. Ten
minutes later, the general found himself in the corridor. The Pope's requirements were clear, too

clear. An open-topped jeep, a tour through the seedier parts of the old city and visits to two of the outlying shanty towns of the Pope's choosing. The day to end with a visit to the seminary for student priests and a private meeting with the country's hierarchy. The following day to follow the same pattern with visits to other slum areas and ending with another meeting with the hierarchy. Otherwise the Pope would make immediate arrangements to leave and the General knew what that would mean. The General knew very well indeed. It would mean a colossal snub for the ruling junta in the world's eyes. It would fuel demands for a change and Xerces Caracco would be out of a job - at the very least.

Uvantes took the news badly but he had to concede. It was unthinkable that the Pope should cut short his much-publicised visit. The President decided against accompanying Leo on his new itinerary. Instead, he busied himself preparing a Press statement to the effect that he was responsible for rearranging the schedule to show the world that he was not afraid to let the Pope see the conditions which, very soon, would be alleviated by his government.

***

The stench was well-nigh unbearable. TV could convey the scene but not the smell. Ramshackle wooden houses leaned on each other for support in a never-ending sea of misery. Open sewers ran down the middle of tracks which passed for roads. The hastily white painted papal jeep had to stop on the outskirts and the Pope continued on foot with Peter Dunne through the laughing, cheering, weeping throng. The sun beat down. Insects buzzed everywhere. The filth was appalling but it did not matter on that day. The Pope had come to the people. He had not come in a sleek limousine but standing on a jeep so all could see him. Priests and aid workers who had toiled for years against poverty, deprivation and police brutality, went down on their knees with the rest and yelled until they could yell no more. Then, in a space to one side of the sprawling mess they called a village, the Pope had mounted the jeep again. His soutane was no longer white but grey from the dust and the pawing of countless hands. His face was burnt from the sun and someone had given him a broad-brimmed hat to protect him. He spoke to them of hope. He spoke for an hour without notes. Then he had to leave. The jeep carried him to a helicopter and he was gone on his way to another similar village two hundred miles away.

Wednesday, 20 December 1978

Carelli eased his feet out of his velvet slippers and crossed his ankles on the low coffee table. He was sunk so low in the armchair that Peter had difficulty seeing him. They were in Peter's bedroom at the Nunciature.

'What a day, eh Peter?' Carelli had abandoned his cloak and cupped a mug of hot coffee in his hands. 'How does he keep going? He certainly got what he wanted but I noticed "El Presidente" kept well out of the way.'

'The Holy Father certainly knows how to get what he wants,' said Peter, sitting rather more sedately in the other armchair. Carelli cackled. 'Get what he wants! He had them eating out of his hands. The ordinary Catholics loved him.'

'Do you think he went a little too far, in some of his speeches I mean?' Peter could not altogether share the other's jubilation.

'Too far? What do you mean?' Carelli eased himself up in his chair.

'Well,' Peter felt unsure of himself. 'He did seem to lay it on a bit thick. All that stuff about an oppressive regime and the right of people to freedom, even at the expense of a civil war. The evils of a Fascist state and the virtues of Socialism. It didn't sound quite right.'

'I see what you mean, of course, but don't forget, Peter, these people are oppressed. They needed a message of hope. The Holy Father combined the spiritual weight of the Church with the aspirations of the people. This is an overwhelmingly Catholic country don't forget.'

'That sounds suspiciously like an apologia to me, Eminence.' Peter looked Carelli directly in the eyes and saw that he had stopped smiling. He correctly surmised that Carelli was bringing the considerable intelligence he masked so easily onto the matter under discussion. He decided to make the most of his slight breach of the Cardinal's defences. 'The meeting with the country's bishops tonight was rather strained, I thought. They did not seem too happy with the Holy Father's undoubted triumph with the people.'

Carelli finished his coffee. 'You pose many problems but you will have to let me sleep on them before I decide whether I should advise the Holy Father. Let us meanwhile, trust in God, as he does.' When Carelli left, he was deep in thought. The euphoria of the day had quite departed. It occurred to Peter that he had, perhaps, merely voiced some of the Cardinal's own misgivings.

***

Unknown to Peter, the Papal Nuncio was airing much the same point of view to the Pope himself.

'But surely Monsignor, the poor, the desperately poor people want me to give them a spark of hope?'

The Nuncio, a tired man, older than his years, pondered the best way to put his argument. His job was thankless. The bishops chided him for being too soft with the regime, the generals thought he was a pain in their respective necks.

'Holy Father, we all appreciate the truly uplifting nature of your remarks to our fellow countrymen. I do agree that they need leadership from the Church. Some of the bishops have expressed disquiet, however, that your remarks might be construed by some of the more violent elements and not to put too fine a point on it as incitement to overthrow the government. As your holiness must be aware, if successful, such an uprising would probably result in a regime as far to the Left as the present regime is to the Right. The Church has to tread a very narrow path in this country.'

Spartov smiled his most benign smile. 'I shall certainly keep your words in mind, Monsignor, when I make my farewell address tomorrow.'

As Spartov ushered out the Nuncio, looking, if possible, even more tired, he felt quite pleased with himself. But he would obviously have to be very careful. He had been shaken by the experiences of the last two days. This was truly a corrupt and vicious regime. If it was not for the Church, the poor would have no one to plead their cause. He closed the door and stopped short. What was he thinking? The Church; he was sworn to destroy it and yet it was clearly the only champion of freedom in this country and probably a dozen more like it. Not for the first time Spartov prepared for bed in a confused state of mind. Peter Dunne, Carelli, the other Cardinals and certainly the bishops of this country were all good men although misguided. But were they misguided? Of course, they were. Who believed in a God these days? It was laughable. But they were good men. He fell asleep many hours later, his personal problems still unresolved.

Thursday, 21 December 1978.

El Presidente felt better than he had felt for three days as he watched the white plane skimming away over the sea. He had been dreading the Pope's farewell speech and it had proved to be less militant in tone than most during the papal visit. With a complacent smile he turned to the Nuncio. 'I think everything went very well.' The Nuncio said nothing. He was wondering how far the Pope's message to the people to show restraint in their just demands would patch matters between Church and State in the long run.

20. GRIMALDI AND OTHERS

Friday, 5 January 1979.

Arthur climbed the bare stone steps to the first floor. The plaster was peeling and the only light filtered up from the street door. Little piles of rubbish nestled against the walls. He found a door with a soiled card pinned to the frame. 'Gramaldi,' it said. He knocked. As usual, Lia had furnished the address and Arthur had made the appointment by 'phone.

The door opened a crack. Arthur peered at the crack of light. What appeared to be a portion of a face peered back. 'Signor Grimaldi?' Arthur asked helpfully. No response. The door was on the verge of closing again. Arthur planted his foot against it. 'I telephoned – Mr Smith – Lia Otello recommended you.' Arthur and the crack regarded each other for a few seconds more. Suddenly, the door opened and Arthur found himself confronted by a small, stooped, grey-haired man whose face consisted largely of pebble glasses. He wore a creased leather apron over a faded blue suit.

'May I come in?' Arthur walked into the room, the little man giving way reluctantly.

'You were not very specific on the telephone.' Nicotine-stained teeth showed briefly as the man demonstrated the power of speech.

'It doesn't do to be too specific on the 'phone. Can we sit?' The question was more than a polite enquiry. At first glance, there appeared to be nowhere in the room to accommodate even one chair. Oddments of all kinds were stacked all over the floor, periodicals, piles of clothes, tools of various descriptions and cartons overflowing with strangely-shaped pieces of metal.

'Come into the office.' Arthur followed Grimaldi into what he took to be a large cupboard. There was just room for a small desk and two chairs, one either side. Arthur selected a chair, first brushing the remains of Grimaldi's breakfast from the seat. Grimaldi shuffled around to the vacant chair and sat down with difficulty in the confined space. A year-old poster advertising the Arts Festival clung hesitantly to the wall above his head.

'I've got friends,' he said inexplicably.

'I'm sure you have,' said Arthur, wondering if this was really the superb craftsman Lia had said. 'Now, let's get down to business.'

'Friends are good things to have, sometimes.' Grimaldi gave the last word peculiar emphasis. 'Best to get the position clear.' It was anything but clear to Arthur but he thought it best to ignore it.

'I understand that you can undertake certain work in absolute secrecy.' Arthur leaned forward to see Grimaldi's reaction.

'Certain work,' Grimaldi rolled the words over his tongue and, with maddening slowness, lit a cigarette. 'Yes, I do certain work,'

'To be precise, can you make me two number plates'

'I have some in stock somewhere.' Grimaldi looked vacantly around the dirty grey walls as if summoning a minion staggering under a load of number plates. No one appeared.

'I do not require any old number plates. I want some very special car registration plates, these are the numbers He took a paper from his pocket book and pushed it at Grimaldi.

'The letters must be gold on a silver background. Can you do it?'

Grimaldi glanced at the paper without interest. 'Fifty thousand lire,' he said.

'I think twenty thousand would be more reasonable and I shall require them in three weeks.'

'You drive a hard bargain, Signor Smith, also a very unusual car.' Grimaldi's stare was less vacant. 'Thirty thousand lire and they will be ready in four weeks.'

'Arthur considered the matter. Four weeks would be cutting things very fine indeed, but Grimaldi, crazy as he seemed, was immovable. Lia had said that he was the very best. Arthur came to a decision. 'Very well. It is understood, of course, that you will carry out this commission with absolute secrecy.' Arthur was beginning to feel a twinge of unease, although Lia had promised that Grimaldi was completely trustworthy.

'Signor Smith.' The pebble glasses had already glazed over. 'I have many secrets. If I used all my knowledge I would be very rich. I would also be very dead. My business depends upon my ability to be silent.' Grimaldi seemed surprised at hearing his own voice. He paused as if mentally selecting the correct phrase. 'My ability,' he repeated, apparently losing interest in the conversation.

Arthur felt for his pocket book. 'I will pay ten thousand lire now, the rest when you complete the work.'

'You know, I could have them ready tomorrow.' Grimaldi offered his nicotine-stained teeth once more for inspection. 'But I am not going to. If you wait you will appreciate it all the more.' He wiped his hands on the front of the leather apron, transferring a shower of metal filings to the table before he reached out and took the notes, which he stowed away in his pocket.

Arthur resisted the temptation to make any remark, the stronger temptation to smash his fist into Grimaldi's face. He got up. He picked his way between the stacks of rubbish in the outer room and reached the corridor. His last impression, as he descended the grubby steps, was being watched all the way to the street by a crack in the door. He felt uneasy about Grimaldi, but there was no alternative but the trust him, for the moment anyhow.

Saturday, 6 January 1979.

Was it a flurry of cardinals? No, a conclave of cardinals surely. But a conclave suggested a particular occasion. A college of cardinals? Technically correct but somehow unsuitable; a mustering perhaps? Peter Dunne speculated idly as he surveyed the flurry, conclave, college or mustering of cardinals in the Sistine chapel. Leo was resplendent in white and gold cope and mitre. He was intoning the agenda for the Synod due to commence in a week's time. The proceedings were being conducted in Latin and Leo was speaking from a portable throne set up in front of the altar. The whole business would be repeated again, for the benefit of the bishops, tomorrow. The cardinals were being given the precedence due to their rank. Every spare minute until the Synod started was being devoted to preparation. Leo was seeing each cardinal and bishop individually for a few minutes. It was a mammoth task.

Wednesday, 10 January 1979.

Franco Esseppi was becoming aware that he was being watched. Each time he ventured out of the

Vatican, his footsteps were dogged by a succession of dark-coated impersonal young men. The whole point about tailing someone is that the someone should not sense that they are being watched. Once they become suspicious, it is relatively easy to check. The gardener had checked, several times. He had deviated from his usual route, only to find that one of the impersonal young men deviated also. He had spent an hour in an unaccustomed trattoria, only to see the same young man waiting when he emerged.

The old man was frightened, but he dare not confide his fears since he knew that the Russians would view the matter as the end of his usefulness. It might, no, it would, lead to unpleasant consequences. So, instead of telling Spartov or passing a message through the seed merchant, he obtained a gun. He was not sure what he intended to do with it, but he felt better with it in his pocket. He had never had a gun before. He did not know even how to fire it properly. It was his second mistake.

21. VISITS

Tuesday, 23 January 1979.

The morning was crisp and cold. Traces of frost still clung like sparkling crystals in sheltered places. Arthur and Maurice stood with a group of dedicated tourists in St Peter's piazza. The piazza was more crowded than usual for the time of year although the doors of the great basilica were shut for the duration of the Synod. It was in its second week. Most of the tourists had collected near the gate of the Bells, through which car after car sped, each with its payload of cardinals and bishops. A steady trickle of bishops, who had elected to walk, picked their way through the tourists towards the archway under the extreme left of the façade. A few taxis stopped just before the entrance to the piazza (and to the Vatican City State).

Maurice shivered despite his warm overcoat and stamped his feet on the unyielding stone. Arthur shivered. They both wore cameras slung around their necks. Arthur nudged Maurice with his elbow. 'There he is.' Maurice watched as an elderly man, dressed in red and muffled in a heavy cloak, stepped out of a taxi and stooped to pay the fare. They had watched Bishop Horniev arrive every day of the Synod. It was essential, said Arthur, to get to know his appearance on sight. The old Bishop made his way unsteadily to join the stream of black cars and red bishops filing through the arch to the sacristy beyond. Now and then the little group of reporters would break ranks to surround one of the arrivals. Bishop Pevier of Marseilles, smiled, held up his hand and passed on his way; Bishop Escivito of Lima, put his head down and ploughed through the questioners. The bluff and red-faced Bishop of Philadelphia stopped and exchanged a few words, laughed, slapped reporters on their backs but declined to pass any comment on the proceedings, 'The Holy Father will speak the mind of the Church in due course.' Several black-robed representatives of non-Catholic churches arrived looking expectant. They received much attention from the journalists but with equally futile results.

'Give us a break, Reverend, the world is waiting for some information about the way things are going in there. Are the Churches nearer unity would you say?' The speaker was a middle-aged man with a microphone sprouting from his hand and a recorder over his arm. The young Methodist minister smiled.

'The discussions are going very well.'

'Can you give me a quote?'

'Do you speak Latin?'

'No.'

'Then I can't give you a quote – the discussions are carried on in Latin you see.'

'I know that but ...' The young minister waved his hand, having won precious metres and vanished through the archway.

'We'd be just as well interviewing the statues around the colonnade.' A colleague put an arm on the reporter's shoulder. 'Even better interviewing two beers, what do you say? We'll make our own quotes, we usually do anyway. They drifted off, looking better.

Nobody stopped Bishop Horniev. Arthur and Maurice made their way out of the piazza and turned down the Via delle Conciliazione on their way to the English College. Having crossed the river, they turned into the Via de Moserrato. Maurice shrugged out of his coat to reveal the black suit and clerical collar of a priest. Arthur walked on to where he had left the Fiat parked around the corner. Maurice paused until he was out of sight and pressed a door bell in the wall under a sign which read: 'Ven. Collegio Inglesi.' Somewhere in the interior of the building he heard the tinkle of a bell. He stamped up and down on the cold step for several minutes. It was an old building and opened directly off the pavement. Suddenly, one of the double doors opened and a dark-haired young man in a black cassock appeared. He was large and muscular, but traces of acne around his chin betrayed his recent transition to manhood. 'Can I help you?' he asked in English. Maurice put on his most beguiling smile.

'I sincerely hope so,' he said, labouring his French accent. 'Am I in time to catch Bishop Horniev?' Maurice, of course, already knew the answer to that question.

The young man frowned. 'I'm terribly sorry. He left for the Synod about an hour ago.' Maurice looked deflated.

'I'm sorry myself. My name is Pierre Lavoire.'

'Do step inside for a moment, Father.' Maurice followed the young man into the scarcely less cold hallway. A staircase ran up at the back of the hall and a corridor ran along behind it, disappearing at either side. Two dark wood chairs stood against the wall. They did not look as though they were there for sitting on. The wall itself was hung with a clutter of pious pictures of ancient vintage, among which Leo had pride of place alongside an engraving of the only English Pope: Adrian IV. Maurice drank it all into his brain. He had trained himself to notice a multitude of details in a few seconds. He turned to the young man who looked eager to please.

'I should explain that I met Bishop Horniev several years ago, while on a visit to Czechoslovakia. I am travelling in Italy and, knowing he was in Rome for the Synod, I thought I would renew the acquaintance. I doubt though, that he would remember me after all this time.'

The young man grinned. He may not remember you, but I am sure he would be delighted to see you again. He is a very sweet old gentleman, although not in the best of health. Could you perhaps return tonight? I am sure the College would be delighted to have you to dinner?'

'Unfortunately, I am heading south immediately after lunch.' Maurice assumed an air of disappointment. Suddenly he brightened. 'Will the Bishop be in, say, a week or ten days, after the Synod ends?'

'Why yes, I believe that he intends to have a week's holiday here in Rome when it is all over. It is very tiring work apparently. I'm sure you could catch him at home any evening after dinner. We eat at seven. Unless I can press you to come early and eat with us?'

'You are really too kind, but I cannot impose upon you, in any case I do not know precisely when I shall be arriving and I shall have only about an hour between trains.'

'Well that's settled then, give us a ring if you like, before you come, just to make sure that the Bishop is free.'

With renewed thanks and promises to give the Bishop the message, Maurice was shown out. As the door closed, Maurice congratulated himself on successfully accomplishing the first stage of the plan. He hurried along the street to Arthur's waiting car.

Wednesday, 24 January 1979.

The seed shop was crowded and Esseppi hung back, examining the racks of packets, tins and implements. The interior of the shop was quite small. Its single window was crammed with Plant pots, fibre glass urns and garden tools. The glass was covered with white paste writing indicating special offers.

The last customer, a little Italian carrying a large plant of indeterminate species which threatened to strangle him, finally staggered out of the shop. The proprietor closed the door after him and wiped his greasy hands on his thinning hair, bringing them down to smooth his very full moustache. His toilet accomplished, he went back behind the stout wooden counter.

Esseppi moved from his scrutiny of the garden implements and approached the counter, fumbling in his pocket for the week's message as he went. He passed the brightly coloured packet over the counter and the other's greasy palm slapped down on it; at the same time placing a bundle of notes on the deeply scored teak with his free hand.

It was at this inauspicious moment that the two men from the Departmento di Pubblica Sicurezza burst into the shop brandishing revolvers and identification badges. Mangini had grown weary of waiting for something to happen and decided to force the pace.

All might have been well. The proprietor had dropped his hand containing the packet below the level of the counter top the moment he heard the door opening. When he saw the guns, he flicked the packet into a pile of waste paper and cartons strewn around his feet. Esseppi turned around and saw the men. He recognised them instantly as part of the team which had trailed him on his expeditions outside the Vatican wall. They had guns. The guns were pointing at him. He was old and his mind wandered but he was in no doubt why the men had come. His cover was blown and he knew it. He dropped the notes and tried to draw his own gun from his raincoat pocket. He got it out no further than the handle.

The noise of gunfire in a small room is deafening. The two detectives had seen the gun at the same time. In fairness it must be said that they tried to aim low. The gardener was standing in front of the seed merchant. Two bullets hit him in the side simultaneously, they shredded his kidney and flung him against the counter facing the merchant. His free hand gripped the wooden top as his legs buckled under him. His other hand, still holding the gun halfway out of his pocket, went into spasm, sending its missile hurtling into the merchant's ample stomach.

The merchant grabbed at his belly, from which bright red blood had suddenly begun to pour in the most alarming way. His eyes stared with horror at Esseppi as he collapsed against the metal shelving and slid to the floor behind the counter, bringing seed packets and bottles of fertilizer cascading down with him. He lay twisting and squirming with the red-hot agony which would not go away.

Esseppi had sunk to his knees, one hand on the counter, the other still clinging to the half-drawn gun. His left side was wet with old man's watery blood.

'What a mess,' hissed one of the two men, while the other sped quickly across the shop to telephone for an ambulance.

Two hours later, the seed merchant was in the mortuary. The gardener, though older, was tougher. The surgeons of San Paolo Hospital worked on him for four hours. He would not live, but he might live long enough to give valuable information.

He lay in a coma. Renaldo Mangini was by his bedside, waiting for him to awake. A very disagreeable search was being made among the mess of paper, sawdust, blood and fertilizer on the floor of the seed shop for the message which Mangini knew had been passed. He had virtually no case against either man, no excuse for the killings unless the message could be found. His job hung on a thread and that thread was very likely the old man's life. Mangini was cold with anxiety, despite the oppressive warmth of the ward, as he stared at the shrivelled figure in the bed surrounded by a mass of electronic equipment monitoring each vital function.

***

Someone had once told Peter Dunne that the letters in mosaic around the interior of the base of Michelangelo's great dome on St Peter's basilica were two metres tall. He had always found it easy to believe. They did not look two metres tall, but then the whole interior of the building was out of scale – as though the builder had built everything three times as big as intended. It was only when the huge building was crowded with people that it was possible to comprehend the vastness of it. Peter, unfashionably, thought it was rather a failing on Michelangelo's part.

From his place behind one of the colossal central piers, he had a wonderful view of proceedings in the basilica. It was crowded in the very special way that he would not see again in his lifetime. Rank upon rank of cardinals, bishops, abbots and representatives of Churches from all over the world, Catholic and non-Catholic, filled the nave to overflowing. He wondered what would happen to the Church if Michelangelo's structural abilities proved to be as poor as his sense of scale and the basilica collapsed at that moment killing everyone inside. Would the

Church grind to a standstill? It could not of course. It would be a terrible nuisance but that would be about all. There were still plenty of bishops who, for one reason or another, had not come to the Synod. No doubt they would elect a new pope and that would be that. What was that bit in the bible about the gates of hell not prevailing?

Mass was coming to a close. It was being concelebrated by six newly ordained and very nervous priests. Monsignor Enrico Donetti, the papal Master of Ceremonies, was flitting about, nudging here and beckoning there. He was an old man, much older than the Pope himself, an expert on the intricacies of papal ceremonial and ecclesiastical precedence. He had served four popes and he was probably the only one in the basilica who really knew what to do next. Compared with the clinically precise English ceremonial in, say, Westminster Abbey – the Queen's Coronation scenes immediately came to mind – the scene in St Peter's was a shamble. Clergy and altar servers milled around in apparent, and possibly real, confusion.

The whole effect was typically Italian. It reminded Peter of the advice an old and worldly-wise priest had given him shortly after ordination: 'Always look as though you know what you're doing and don't smoke in the chancel.' They did not all look as though they knew what they were doing but, at least, no one was smoking, not that he could see anyway. He assumed it was all incense? He had grown to prefer the Italian way of doing ceremonial. There was something friendly about it. He settled into a more comfortable position on his knees. Realising that he was pandering to bodily comforts instead of mortifying the flesh, he tried to resume his uncomfortable position, failed.

It was cold in the basilica. How many of the more elderly clergy would catch pneumonia? Probably the Holy Spirit kept an eye on things like that.

The ceremony was drawing to a close. Leo was standing in front of the throne to give the papal blessing, A little group of black and white figures clustered around him. One was holding the book – a huge thick red volume for so few words that the Pope knew by heart anyway, another held a stick microphone trembling slightly, whether due to nerves or the cold he was not sure, another held the papal crosier, the shepherd's staff, the whole assembly knelt

'Benedicat vos Omnipotens Deus.' Leo's voice was wonderfully strong, if not very musical. 'Pater et Filius et Spiritus Sanctus.' His large square hand traced the cross three times.

'Amen.' The response swelled and filled the church. Then the Pope was making his way on foot down the centre of the nave and then to the Vatican Palace adjoining. Peter hurried after the procession which was slow enough due to Leo's habit, which

Spartov of course copied, of stopping frequently to exchange a few words with some of the prelates lining the nave. Peter, having caught up with Leo, kept close behind because he knew that, once the Pope had left, the crush to get to the sacristy would be enormous.

When Peter finally reached the Pope's private sacristy in the Vatican Palace, he found the Pope with a worried frown on his face, still partly vested and listening with close attention to one of the papal functionaries. Spartov looked up as he entered.

'Peter we must go out.' It was the first time the Pope had addressed Peter by his Christian Name and he guessed it must be a slip of the tongue. The Pope was very punctilious in some things, particularly if they affected others, casual about himself. He obviously had something weighty on his mind. 'I have just received some bad news. One of the gardeners, he has been here at the Vatican for many years, is seriously ill at San Paolo hospital here in the city. It seems he has been shot.' Peter noticed that Leo looked unusually agitated.

'Do you think it would be better to let me go and see him? I could let you have the details when I got back.'

'No Monsignor, I am the pastor of my flock and this old man has a claim upon my time. I have spent several hours in conversation with him in the gardens.' Spartov wondered if he was going too far, but he had to know how much Esseppi had said. Fortunately, Peter seemed to accept it as just another of the Pope's well-known kindly actions.

Within an hour, the papal car had deposited Spartov at the doors of the hospital, this time accompanied by police outriders in approved fashion. The senior staff had been alerted and Spartov together with Peter were quickly whisked up through the white tiled corridors to the third floor. On the way up in the lift the surgeon explained that the old gardener would almost certainly not survive more than a few hours. He was unconscious but they were hopeful that he would regain consciousness shortly because the Security People wanted to interview him.

Spartov looked grim as he was shown into the Intensive Care Unit. Mangini sprang to his feet in astonishment. He was probably the only person in the hospital who did not know the Pope was coming. Spartov glanced at the grey face on the pillow. The eyes were flickering. 'Has he spoken yet?'

'No Holy Father, we were hoping, but if he dies without regaining consciousness, we will lose much valuable information. Mangini looked apologetic.

Spartov knew that Esseppi had the power to expose him and probably would in these circumstances. He decided to play his trump card.

The Pope became stern. 'If he dies now, who knows but that he may lose his immortal soul? That is the most important thing to me and certainly to him now. You must leave me in case he wishes to confess.'

'But, Your Holiness.' Mangini could see that the grey eyelids were flickering more rapidly. 'I must stay.'

Spartov turned the full voltage of his blue eyes on the unfortunate detective. 'You must go. When We have attended to the affairs of his soul, you can interview him if the doctor allows it. If you feel inclined to argue, we will remind you that this man is a citizen of the Vatican State and We are his Sovereign.'

Mangini hesitated. He was unsure of the legal position and there was no time to find out. He knew that he could not argue with this formidable man. He left the room, the doctor and Peter followed. Spartov hesitated. Clearly Esseppi had said nothing incriminating so far. He was on the point of death. Equally clearly, he was rapidly regaining consciousness. Spartov knew what he had to do. In Esseppi's present state, a pillow over his head would quickly induce heart failure without the need for suffocation which would leave traces. He bent over the bed and took hold of the pillow. At that moment, Esseppi's eyes opened. He gazed uncomprehendingly for a second and then he smiled. Spartov stopped, hands resting on the pillow. Esseppi spoke. 'Holy Father, you are so kind, will you do one last thing for me?'

Outside the door, Mangini was protesting to the impassive surgeon, who seemed to be enjoying the situation. Peter realised, with a start, that he was still holding the case containing the impedimenta of Viaticum which the Pope would need if, as seemed likely, he was about to administer the last rites. He hesitated. He did not want to break into the middle of the old man confessing his sins, but it was unlikely that he had fully regained consciousness. He took only a few moments to make up his mind. He knocked once and stepped into the room.

Pope Leo was bent over the bed. The old man was lying with his eyes fully open staring. He caught a few words, meaningless. '…a real priest, you must grant me that.'

Leo turned at the sound of the door, smoothing the old man's pillow. Peter put the case at the foot of the bed and turned to go out of the room again. Leo called him back. 'I think you had better attend him. He seems to prefer it and we must respect his wishes.'

Spartov left Peter in the room and stood in the corridor. Every instinct told him that he was making a mistake but he could not help himself. Esseppi knew the truth. Spartov had never been properly ordained a priest of course and Esseppi knew it and wanted a real priest, someone he believed could forgive sin. Spartov wondered what he would tell Peter. Then he realised. No one would ever know because in the Catholic Church the seal of the confessional was absolute and the priest hearing the confession had a solemn duty to act as if he had been told nothing and to make every effort to forget what the penitent had said.

But Mangini was a different matter. The old man would surely tell him everything. How would they set about getting rid of him? Presumably they would try and avoid a scandal, suggest he went into a monastery. What if Spartov stood firm and denied everything? His thoughts were interrupted by a door opening. Spartov realised that he had been standing against the wall, staring at the floor. Probably the others assumed he was deep in prayer. Collect himself, panic must be avoided, he still carried plenty of weight.

Mangini sprang forward as Peter appeared. 'Can I go in now? It really is most urgent.'

'You can certainly go in but it will do you no good. The old man died as I finished Viaticum.' Peter looked tired. Mangini pushed him aside and sprinted into the room, followed by the surgeon. Spartov stood at the door as the surgeon quickly examined Esseppi and confirmed that nothing could be done.

'It's a miracle he lasted as long as he did,' he remarked cheerfully, adding, 'Begging your pardon,' as he remembered that the Pope was standing nearby. 'I didn't mean...'

Mangini was almost hysterical. 'Try, try anything. Surely you can resuscitate him long enough to give me the information I need, drugs, all this equipment.' Mangini waved a despairing hand at the humming, clicking, cold electronics.

'I can't and even if I could I would not. A man should be able to die in dignity. Would you care to have to die twice, when your time comes?' The surgeon turned to Spartov. 'Was it not one of your illustrious predecessors who stated that we need not strive "officiously" to keep someone alive?'

'Indeed, it was.' Spartov vaguely remembered it from one of his lectures at Linanka. He was once more master of the situation. Whatever Esseppi had confessed to Peter would remain secret and the gardener himself was now forever beyond the clutches of the Security Department. Mangini wandered absently out of the room and down the corridor. He had a curious floating sensation which he thought might be the beginning of a nervous breakdown. He rather hoped it was.

Spartov did as he knew was expected and knelt in an attitude of prayer beside the bed. He took the opportunity to thank the old man's God for his excellent timing. He also prayed, to no god in particular, for a way out of his problems. Things were beginning to go wrong. Much depended upon what Peter Dunne did next.

Spartov got to his feet and signed a blessing over the corpse. He wondered if Peter knew that he was play acting. Yet it did not seem like play acting. On that cold February night, in the stuffy green-walled room, crammed with banks of impotent technical equipment, something very strange was happening to Andrei Spartov.

On the way back in the car, he turned to Peter. 'I will say my Mass tomorrow morning for the repose of his soul. Had he any relatives?'

'I think he had a sister somewhere, they are trying to contact her.'

'Good, if they get in touch with her tonight and she feels able, tell her that she will be welcome to attend my Mass tomorrow.'

'That is very kind, Holy Father.' Peter looked troubled.

'No, not kind, I think of this man as representing my flock.'

'Holy Father.'

'Yes.' Spartov detected an unusual note in Peter's voice and prepared himself for the worst.'

I know of course, that what passed between the old man and myself is under the seal of confession.'

'It is indeed and you must put it out of your mind.' Spartov felt a moment of panic. Was Peter going to break the seal and confront him? He must be dissuaded at all costs.

'But, Holy Father, the man has presented me with a problem and, as Christ's Vicar on Earth, only you can advise me.' Spartov was startled. Peter was addressing him in no uncertain manner as the genuine Pope and yet would he do that if Esseppi had told him the truth. He decided to take a chance.

'If you can put your problem in the broadest terms, without revealing what the old man said, I will do my best to help you.'

Peter was obviously unsure what he ought to say. 'The best way I can explain it is to say that I know that when a man is dying, he is often delirious and says things which are probably fantasy. Yet, if that same man charges me to reveal what he has said to some civil authority, should I comply?'

Spartov relaxed slightly. Clearly Peter could not bring himself to believe whatever it was that the gardener had told him.

'I think I can answer your question best by asking you in turn to ask yourself this question: By complying with the old man's wishes, would you be performing any worthwhile action and, most of all, can you comply without revealing the man' sin? If the answer to either question is "no", then you should put the matter out of your mind.'

'I think that I had better try to put the whole thing out of my mind,' said Peter. Doing it was another matter.

Friday, 2nd February 1997.

Spartov sat, flanked by senior cardinals, facing the vast assembly of prelates and lay experts. They were gathered in the capacious beige-decorated Hall of Audiences, erected for Paul VI in 1971 by the Italian architect Nervi. It was the last day of the Synod. Four full sessions had assembled to hear speeches by men from all corners of the world. Spartov had made a point of meeting each one for a short conversation.

Spartov had spent the night before the great day in his private chapel. Not out of piety, but because he could not face the prospect of tossing in his bed. His chapel was the one other place where he was unlikely to be disturbed. He badly needed to think things out. He had been trained for years and finally placed in this special position. It gave him a unique opportunity to sabotage the Synod and bring disarray to the whole Christian world. All the major Churches had sent representatives and an indeterminate, or better a negative, outcome would be disastrous. That would serve his masters best. There was no doubt where his duty lay. Unfortunately, he had had time to absorb the atmosphere of the Church. Time to discover that it was not the corrupt organisation he had been led to expect. Could there possibly be a God? It seemed a shattering concept. If there was ….?

The Christian ethic of returning evil with good and putting faith in some sort of Supreme Being was that all it was? It was in his power to destroy the Roman Catholic Church or at least severely weaken it and then the whole Christian world might divide upon itself. Why did he hesitate?

Only Spartov had all the reports from the working parties. Only he had seen that, incredibly, they were unanimous in advocating the way forward through unity.

He could meld the reports into one harmonious document or he could reshape the words to foment divisions. It would be possible, easy, to insert a word here and a phrase there to make his final summing up an instrument for the destruction of unity. The Church would listen if the Pontiff said that the movement towards unity was premature. Some would dissent and the rot would begin. Spartov had only an hour's sleep before it was time for his Mass.

Spartov riffled the stiff papers on his knees. Monsignor Donetti adjusted the position of the microphone although it needed no adjustment. Spartov sat with head bowed. His eyes had heavy bags, his cheeks were puffy with fatigue. The elderly cardinal from Milan broke into a fit of coughing which seemed to emphasise the absolute silence in the Hall. Peter, from his customary seat to one side of the gathering, eyed Spartov with apprehension, desperately trying to banish the gardener's dying confession from his mind. The gates of Hell shall not prevail,' he kept telling himself, trying to blot out what he knew. He realised he was trembling and hoped no one noticed. Spartov looked up. He seemed to have aged ten years in one night. He looked like a spectre, white face and snow-white hair. Peter felt helpless to prevent what his heart told him and his mind rejected, was to be the death knell of the Church.

Spartov cleared his throat and began to read from his laboriously prepared speech

***

Arthur Brown knocked at the almost bare wood of the door. After an age, the door opened a crack.

'Signor Grimaldi, Smith again, you remember me?'

The door closed and, after a period of rattling safety chain, it opened again. This time wide enough to reveal the leather-aproned, pebble-glassed figure of Grimaldi. 'Come in,' he said.

Arthur stood amongst the clutter of the outer room and watched the grey-haired man rummaging aimlessly among the cardboard cartons. He looked up at Arthur. 'Can I help you?'

Arthur looked at the bland, uncomprehending face with incredulity. 'What do you mean? Don't you remember me? Smith, I called and ordered some license plates, special ones. You were going to have them ready.'

'Number plates.' Grimaldi screwed up his eyes behind the thick lenses. He smiled slyly. I get a lot of orders for license plates. What was the number?'

Perhaps Grimaldi really was as stupid as he appeared. That could be good or bad. If he had forgotten to make them... Arthur broke out in a sweat. He leaned forward and hissed. 'It was a plate with gold letters on a silver ground. There is only one like it.'

'Ah,' Grimaldi turned back to ransacking the cartons. An old starting handle was extricated from one. It was placed carefully aside. After a few minutes Arthur could stand it no longer.

'Are you going to give them to me or have you lost them you stupid old man? Did you ever make them?'

'Come into the office.'

They went once more into the tiny office. Arthur noticed that the poster had finally relinquished its tenuous hold on the wall and lay unheeded on the floor. A tattered cardboard box stood on the table. Grimaldi reached inside and took out a long flat package. He passed it to Arthur and stood, one hand on his hip, the other tapping a stubbly chin.

Arthur unwrapped the package and held the two gleaming license plates. He looked at Grimaldi in astonishment. 'You had them in here the whole time.'

Stupid old men can't be too careful, Signor Smith.'

'That's true I suppose. These plates are excellent.'

'Good, it was difficult to get the letters without exciting suspicion, so I had to make each one. They are not solid gold of course. Special care went into their making, yes, special care.' He appeared to be going off into a trance again. Arthur decided to be brisk.

'Here is the rest of the money.' He pushed a parcel of notes across the table. Grimaldi stowed them away in the cardboard box without looking at them. Arthur turned to go. He had reached the outer door when he felt the old man's hand on his arm. 'Yes, what is it?'

'I hope they give every satisfaction and are suitable for the purpose for which they are intended.'

'Yes, yes, thank you.' Arthur extricated himself with difficulty and almost ran out of the room. He stopped before he went out of the street door and walked calmly to his car, parked in the alley around the corner. Rex was waiting for him.

'Did you get what you wanted?'

'Yes but...'

'But what?'

'I'm not sure about the old man.'

'Why?' Rex stared straight ahead at the occasional pedestrian passing the end of the alley.

'He's either a fool or very clever. If he's clever, he poses no threat. A fool is different. He might talk. Maybe he already has.' Arthur felt better now, away from the crazy world of Grimaldi; and he had the plates. 'Proceed as we discussed.' Rex simply nodded and started to get out of the car. 'Wait, he stuffed the money into a cardboard box he has on the table in a little office. You'd better get that, if you can. Don't forget, it should look like an accident.'

'I haven't much experience with accidents, all my clients were intended.' Before Arthur could reply, Rex left the car and, carrying only an old brown paper bag, he strolled down the alley to the block of old apartments. He paused for a second on the threshold, hefted the bag to a more comfortable position and mounted the steps to Grimaldi's door.

He knocked and the door opened its customary crack. 'Mr Smith asked me...; That was as far as he got. The door slammed shut and Rex heard the sound of bolts being shot. Rex stepped back and kicked at the lock with the sole of his boot. The door splintered a little, but held. He kicked again. The door disintegrated into a tangle of rotten wood, still held at the hinges and the bolts, top and bottom. Rex forced his way through the mass of splintered wood and half fell into the room. Grimaldi stood, frozen in front of the piles of rubbish, arms up in front of his head.

A knife appeared as if by magic in Rex's hand. Without hesitation, he plunged it up to the handle into Grimaldi's stomach. The old man fell to his knees, his arms clasped now about his middle. 'Were the goods not ... satisfactory?'

Rex stared at him. 'Sure,' he said and then boot kicked him amongst the stacks of cardboard boxes.

He looked around and saw two doors. The first one led into a sophisticated workshop, equipped with lathes, saws and drills. In one corner stood an electrical furnace. He tried the other door. The cardboard box still stood on the table. It was the work of a moment to find the wad of notes. Rex came back into the outer room. There was no movement from the pile of cartons which had fallen over Grimaldi. He stooped down and took a tin of petrol from the carrier bag and emptied its contents on the floor. He retreated to the shattered door. He could hear movements somewhere in the building. He waited until the noise stopped then struck a match and tossed it onto the pool of petrol. The resulting flash took him by surprise and flung him out onto the landing. The door opposite opened at that moment and a woman appeared. She was large and fat and screaming.

'Quick. Fire!' yelled Rex in English and bolted down the steps, leaving the woman shrieking at the raging inferno that had been Grimaldi's apartment.

Arthur had heard the explosion and the Fiat was waiting in the street outside with the door open and engine running. Rex staggered inside.

'For God's sake get down, you're black,' shouted Arthur and, with a protesting screech, the wheels finally gripped the shiny cobbles and the car shot off down the street.

Arthur closed the shutter before allowing Rex out of the car.

'Get upstairs and clean yourself down.'

After Rex had gone into the apartment, Arthur opened the shutter again and drove the Fiat to the other side of the city. He left it parked and locked in a quiet street and made his way back to the apartment by bus and taxi, finally walking the last half mile. It was raining when he got back and it was very late. He fell into a chair. Lia brought him a whiskey. 'Is everything alright?' Arthur loosened his collar where the rain had soaked through. 'No, I'm afraid not. Where is that cretin?'

'I'm here.' Rex stood in the doorway, not in the least put out. He had showered and changed into another set of his seemingly inexhaustible supplies of old jeans and sweat shirts. The smoke marks had gone but his eye brows were singed. He looked strange. Maurice sat on the sofa, idly playing with a piece of string. 'What happened?'

Arthur answered. 'Rex bungled the Grimaldi job.' Lia gave a start, fear lurking just behind the mascara.

'Grimaldi? What have you done?'

'What have I done? What has Rex here done?'

'But Grimaldi, you haven't hurt him?'

'No, we haven't hurt him. Rex skewered him with his toy and then blew up the apartment with himself in it.' Arthur glared at Rex, fighting hard to retain his composure. 'I wonder why I hired you?'

'Shall I go?' Rex seemed unmoved.

'No, you won't damn well go.' Arthur lost his battle with his composure and banged his glass down on the small table in front of him, gobbets of amber liquid slopping out onto the polished wood. 'Every policeman in Rome will have your description by now. The first thing for you to do is to go and dye your hair and eyebrows, what's left of them, then you stay indoors until I tell you that it's safe to leave.' Lia looked strained. 'Don't you realise who Grimaldi was?'

'A foolish old man who, fortunately, had considerable skill in metalwork.' Arthur, as usual, was angry, not at the activity but, at the amateurish way it had been carried out. 'I thought Rex was an expert.'

Grimaldi was one of the Mafia's most skilled workmen. He was doing this job as a special favour for me. He usually works only for the Mafia.' Lia's face was white with tension. 'I shall be marked for this.'

Arthur looked up at her, his calm had suddenly reappeared. 'A black mark, no doubt, but Grimaldi had to be eliminated. Don't distress yourself, my dear, I think there is a very good chance that Rex will not be recognised, despite what I said, he was only seen by one old woman and he was as black as a coalman. In any case, you will be away from here shortly, free to go anywhere in the world you choose.'

Lia sat down. 'I'm still afraid,' she said. Arthur took command again.

'Yes, well we are all afraid at times, but I see no reason why even your Mafia friends can connect us to the killing. Let's go to bed. It will be a busy day tomorrow, eh Maurice?' Maurice nodded. He was already seeing signs in the others which made him fearful of the outcome of their scheme. Lia was pathologically afraid of the very name 'Mafia,' understandable he supposed. Rex was unmoved by everything except death and then not in the way he should be moved. No remorse, the possibility that he might be caught did not seem to affect him. Perhaps he had a death wish. Arthur appeared outwardly reliable but even his urbane façade crumbled at any sign of a hitch in his plans. But he could improvise. Perhaps all would be well after all. They were much too committed now to turn back anyway. He did not imagine Arthur would allow any backing out at this stage. The thought of relaxing with plenty of money also had its appeal.

***

The applause was spontaneous and thunderous. It went on and on. Peter had never heard anything like it. Tears of joy were visible even on the cheeks of Monsignor Enrico Donetti who must have witnessed much. The Pope, after delivering a message of unity, peace and understanding, had outlined a plan for the future of the Church which could only have one end – the unity of all Christian faiths. Spartov himself sat impassive, utterly worn out. After he had given his blessing, the applause broke out anew, but he seemed not to hear it. He went straight out of the vast hall to his private apartments.

Peter waited in his office for the summons which did not come and, eventually, after ascertaining that the Pope had retired to his room for bed, he went to bed himself, elated at the outcome of the Synod but troubled by the Pope's manner. At the very moment of renewed hope in the future, he seemed like a man without hope himself.

22. DEATH AND KIDNAP

Saturday, 3rd February 1979

It was still raining the following morning when Arthur and Rex arrived at the garage. Arthur swung his silver-topped cane in one hand and carried a briefcase in the other. He was dressed in the black hat of a typical Italian business man. Rex walked uncomfortably by his side, carrying a brown paper parcel. He had dyed his hair black and wore heavy-rimmed spectacles, at Arthur's insistence, to disguise his appearance. He too, was dressed in business clothes and felt strange.

The morning papers had carried a very brief account of the incident at Grimaldi's apartment. There was no mention of Rex having been seen and the report seemed to suggest that the fire was accidental. Forensic tests would certainly show that Grimaldi had been murdered and that the fire had been started with the help of petrol but, for the moment, perhaps for long enough, they were safe. The report had hinted that the deceased had been a recluse who dabbled in explosive materials. There was a certain 'serves him right' feeling in the account.

Arthur looked at the garage doors with a faint sense of disgust. It repelled him to conduct most of his business in this sort of environment. In a few weeks, however, all that would be behind him.

A telephone call to the garage had ascertained that the curly-haired Italian, whose name turned out to be Victor, was in the garage and could fix the plates.

Arthur knocked on a small wicket in the double doors. The sound of a high-speed electric drill stopped and Victor appeared. 'Come in,' he said.

Arthur took a look along the dingy alley, saw nobody and followed Victor inside. Rex walked forward and smacked the bonnet of the Mercedes admiringly. 'Nice motor,' he said. Arthur did not reply. He disliked Rex when he was silent but even more so when he spoke.

He turned to Victor. 'We have brought the plates; will you fix them now? You're not expecting anyone are you?'

'No Signor, my business transactions are mostly done at night.'

'Good, Rex, the plates.' Rex took the parcel from under his arm and handed it to the Italian who took it to a bench at the side of the garage. He unwrapped the plates carefully and looked across at Arthur who still stood by the garage doors.

'These are very special plates.'

'Yes, I know, will you fix them now?' Victor shrugged and selected a screwdriver and screws, he made short work of fixing the plates.

'We want to take the car now. Is the tank full?' Victor was now standing facing Arthur with Rex behind him.

'Yes, it's all ready, key in my pocket. It will cost you another fifty thousand lire – in the circumstances.' He grinned. It was not a pleasant grin.

'I thought it might,' said Arthur. 'We've brought some extra funds, Rex!' Something in his tone alerted the Italian who began to turn in alarm, but Rex was quicker. With a simple forward thrust, like the one he employed for Grimaldi, he drove the knife into Victor's back. Arthur sprang back as Victor's hand clawed at him, his face distorted with pain and rage. Rex put his foot in the small of the Italian's back and pulled the knife clear, sending Victor sprawling over the workbench, blood flowing freely out of the tear in his overalls.

Rex gathered up a couple of sacks and threw them over the body which began to slide off the bench. The sacks soaked up the blood, but they were saturated in seconds as Victor's heart continued to pump. He fell back onto the concrete floor, eyes open, staring at the ceiling, arms by his side, hands jerking, clenching and unclenching. Blood spilled from the sagging mouth and his eyes became glassy. His arms still twitched and the lake of blood continued to spread around the sacking. The whole business had taken less than thirty seconds.

Rex stood, perfectly relaxed and inspected his coat for spots of blood. There were none. He walked over and carefully wiped the knife on an oily rage.

'Goodness, I never realised there was so much blood,' said Arthur, leaning against the garage door. 'I thought you were an expert with a knife.'

'I am,' replied Rex evenly. 'It's more difficult than most people imagine to actually kill with a knife. My way, they simply bleed out and are dead very quickly. There's a knack to getting the blade in cleanly and severing the artery. I like blood.' Arthur understood, with a shock, that Rex was high from the killing.

'What about the key? I'll make sure there are no splashes on the car.'

Rex went through Victor's pockets with less emotion than a butcher cleaning a chicken while Arthur, glad to turn his back on the scene, inspected the car. A fine speckle of red-brown spots, already oxidising, had sprayed the wing. He carefully wiped them off with yet another old rag.

Rex stood up triumphant with the key. Arthur opened his briefcase on the bonnet of the car and took out two fat tubes which he squeezed onto an old saucer he found lying on the workbench and fastidiously mixed the result into a thick goo.

Together, they pulled Victor's body to the back of the garage and covered the pool of blood with more sacking. Rex drew the heavy bolts and opened the doors to let Arthur drive the car out into the street. It was still deserted. He parked it and walked back to help Rex. They shot the bolts home and secured them with liberal applications of the epoxy resin which Arthur had been making. Then they emerged from the wicket door and Arthur locked it with the key Victor had given them on his previous visit. He kicked the key back inside the garage under the door and applied more epoxy resin to the keyhole. 'It will set rock hard and the doors will have to be broken down to get in, if anybody bothers.' Arthur put the saucer containing the remains of the resin into his briefcase and got in the car, heading towards the Trastevere apartment. It was nearly eleven o'clock.

***

Renaldo Mangini returned to his desk and looked around the office. Files filled every conceivable space. He had just returned from a very unpleasant meeting with his superior. Promotion, even his present post, was in danger of slipping away. He rang for the chief of the forensic department who had been attempting to sort out the mess on the floor of the seed merchant's shop for over a week. He knocked on the door in a perfunctory way and came in. He slouched into a chair opposite Mangini and peered with bright black eyes through steel framed spectacles. His grey hair was tousled and he looked short of sleep. An enormous pipe hung dangerously from his mouth.

'What have you got for me, Louis?' Mangini tried to keep the eagerness out of his voice. He failed.

'There.' The old man called Louis tossed a polythene packet onto the desk. Inside, scraps of brownish paper were mounted on a piece of card. 'We found something, but what with the blood and the fertilizer, I doubt whether you can make much of it.'

'I can't make anything of it at all. Is this the best you can do?' Mangini's stomach fell right out through the soles of his shoes.

'Unwrapping that seed packet and getting out the message was worse than deciphering the Dead Sea Scrolls. Now there would have been an interesting job.' Louis became animated for a brief moment before tiredness overtook him.

'But it's unreadable. Can't you bring anything out at all by infra-red or one of your other techniques?' Mangini waved a hand vaguely.

'Well, we did get something.' Louis spoke slowly as if reluctant to admit any success at all. 'All we made out were three words: "Leo", "Synod" and "Carelli."'

'That's all?'

'That's it.'

'Well, at least it shows it to have been a message of some kind relating to Vatican affairs.' Mangini tried to sound cheerful. 'You've been a great help. Thanks.'

Louis got up and tapped out his pipe in Mangini's ash tray. He left, leaving the packet behind. Mangini labelled it "Exhibit B" and put it in a drawer with the earlier message. After a few minutes thought, he summoned the small group of men who were working on the case. When they were assembled, he gave his instructions.

'We have to be very careful. We are not allowed to interfere with the Vatican State unless they request it and, ordinarily, matters like this are notified to them for comment. However, I have a feeling about this and we will keep it to ourselves for the moment, understood?'

The seven men grouped around the desk signified that they understood.

'Good, now here's what we are going to do. Position yourselves as inconspicuously as possible near the entrances to the Vatican. There are only really four, you can forget the galleries. That leaves the Porta di Sant Anna, the Bronze Gate, the Gate of Bells and the service entrance nearby.'

'What are we looking for?' The speaker was one of the men who had shot the gardener. Mangini favoured him with a wintry stare.

'Anything and everything. Carry no guns. Keep a record of all comings and goings. If the old gardener was the only messenger boy, then whoever is wanting the information will try to establish another line of communication to whoever is leaking information in the Vatican. I expect reports on my desk, together with any comments every evening. Agree between you who is going to do the day shift and who the night. Get to it immediately.'

'But we don't know who most of the people are.'

'Put down names when you recognise them, or descriptions – bishop, priest with grey beard, and car numbers. Got it?'

They got it and the unfortunate seven, resigned to weeks of boredom in parked cars, filed out, looking less than enthusiastic.

'Mangini considered whether he should risk putting some kind of 'phone tap on the exchange but decided against it; a decision he would regret. He thought the chances of obtaining what he wanted that way were remote. As an afterthought, he arranged for a watch to be kept on each of the iron curtain embassies and also those of the USA and the UK.

***

Later in the day Maurice departed for a meeting with Bishop Horniev on the pretext that he had just arrived back in Rome for a couple of hours. At about ten o'clock that evening Maurice found himself once again inside the draughty entrance hall of the English College. This time the receptionist was a willowy goggle-eyed student with pale, almost transparent hair.

He explained the purpose of his visit. 'I telephoned earlier,' he said helpfully.

He followed the young man up the nicely carved staircase. At the top, his nostrils were assailed by the unmistakable smell he had grown to associate with monasteries and convents no matter what the country, a kind of holy beeswax. 'Where half a dozen monks or nuns are gathered together, there is ecclesiastical floor polish in the middle of them,' he muttered under his breath. The youth turned.

'Pardon Father?'

'Oh, nothing, I often talk to myself, silly habit.' Maurice smiled to indicate that he was not verging on insanity.

'Bishop Horniev is not really well, Father,' said the goggle-eyed youth.

'Yes, I know, poor man.'

'He's quite bright though for his age.' The youth obviously classed everyone over forty as a candidate for advanced senile decay.

Endless corridors of faltering small talk later, they arrived at a handsome panelled door. It was opened, without ceremony, by the elderly bishop.

Joseph Vladimir Horniev was not an imposing man. He was even smaller and slighter than Maurice had thought when he had seen him in the piazza. His abundant white hair was carefully combed and his face bore the signs of care. A network of fine red blood vessels stood out in sharp relief on his pale cheeks. He was dressed in a simple black cassock with pectoral cross at his chest. His old face broke into a smile when he saw Maurice, watery eyes crinkling at the corners.

'You must be Father Lavoire, do come in and sit down.' The willowy youth melted away and Maurice followed Horniev into a splendidly untidy room, overflowing with books and papers. A bed stood in a recess and two armchairs were drawn up to an electric fire. Horniev waved Maurice into one and settled himself gently into the other. The soft upholstery almost swallowed him.

'I understand, from Michael, that you once knew me. I wonder when that was? I don't want to appear rude but I really cannot place you. My memory, of course, is not what it was.' He spoke in strongly accented French in deference to Maurice. His voice was soft and an air of old world courtesy clung to him like a thick cloud of tobacco smoke

'It's quite understandable, My Lord. You must think my visit a terrible imposition on your time. I only met you once, when I visited your country a few years ago. I was very impressed and I just thought I would call and pay my respects.' Maurice leaned forward as he spoke, to what he hoped was the right degree of priestly earnestness.

'It's all very gratifying, Father, more than I deserve. I'm afraid. As for taking up my time; the Synod is now over and I am taking a short holiday before I return. What a pity you are just passing through Rome. I could have arranged for you to meet the Holy Father. He is an old friend, you know, and he humours my aged requests – more so than I deserve, I'm afraid. I should not presume upon his old friendship. But how are you enjoying your time in Italy? I envy you your energy.' Horniev spoke in a level monotone, changing swiftly from topic to topic. His body might be old, but his mind was sharp, despite his protestations about failing memory.

'I detect an unhappiness behind your face, Father. Everything is not quite as it should be, is that not true?'

Maurice was startled by the last remark. He had expected a doddering, absent-minded fossil, not someone who could almost read his mind.

'We all have doubts at times, my Lord. Perhaps the Synod has resolved some of them for me. My journey is in the nature of a pilgrimage.'

'How I wish you could have met the Holy Father, he has a way of dissolving doubts. I think the Synod has produced a message which will inspire, not only you, but the whole world. Yesterday's meeting and the Holy Father's closing homily was most encouraging.'

Maurice breathed an almost audible sigh of relief. It seemed the Bishop had accepted his explanation. He would be meeting the Holy Father sooner than the good Bishop could have arranged it, if everything went according to plan.

'May I offer you a glass of wine, Father?'

The moment Maurice had been waiting for had arrived.

'That would be delightful my Lord, may I get it to save your legs?'

'Very kind.' Horniev said, half turning. 'Over there in the tall cupboard, Frascati for me. It's a nice decent local wine. I find the heavy wines a little too much for me nowadays.'

Maurice got up and passed behind the Bishop's chair to a tall mahogany piece, by the look of it brought over from England a century before. Probably it had been the prized possession of a long-forgotten Rector, or maybe one of the professors. A few months ago, he would have been bending his talents to separating the cabinet from its present owners, now he scarcely gave the matter more than a passing thought.

'I think there are glasses there,' said Horniev from behind the tall back of the armchair.' 'Yes, everything is fine,' said Maurice. He poured two glasses of the almost clear wine. From his pocket, he took the small bottle given him by Arthur, removed the stopper and poured the contents in one movement. Arthur had assured him that the liquid was virtually tasteless and would take about half an hour to bring on a heart spasm. He hoped it did not finish off the old man or their plan would be postponed yet again. He knew that Arthur would have calculated it very finely and he wondered, not for the first time, what Arthur's original profession had been; a family doctor perhaps.

'When he handed the glass to the Bishop, he noticed that the liquid, whatever it was, had made the wine a little cloudy. The Bishop noticed it too.

'Dear me, are we getting near the bottom of the bottle?' Maurice looked at the glass and at his own, he had no alternative.

'Mine seems clearer, please have it.' He stretched out his hand wondering what he would do if the Bishop accepted.

'No, most certainly not,' Horniev held up his free hand in dismissal of the idea. 'It may be dust at the bottom of the glass. In any case, the host should always give the guest the best he has to offer and save the less good for himself. Good for my soul.' Maurice breathed again and took a sip from his glass, glancing at his watch as he did so. It was half past ten.

'Are you late, Father?' Horniev had noticed the movement. 'I do hope you can stay a little while.'

'I'm afraid that I must leave in about twenty minutes.'

It was just ten minutes to eleven when Maurice stepped out into the cold street. He had stayed until Horniev had finished his wine and then made hurried excuses to leave. He thought it prudent to remark to the goggle-eyed youth that the Bishop had seemed far from well when he left him, although at that time, the drug had no discernible effect. 'I'll see that the Rector is informed,' the youth had assured him. It was almost eleven thirty when Maurice arrived back at the apartment to report that everything had gone smoothly at the English College.

Lia had finished clearing away the remains of their scratch meal and sat on the arm of the sofa, one leg crossed over the other. She smoked a foul-smelling Italian cigarette which seemed to calm her. Rex walked up and down the room. He had not descended from his high of the morning. He had insisted on telling Lia and Maurice all the bloody details over lunch, a procedure which did nothing to help their digestions. It seemed that Rex only became fully alive when he was an instrument of death himself, a sort of latter day vampire.

Sunday, 4th February 1979

Time dragged as they all waited for the next phase to commence. Eventually Arthur looked at his watch. 'One o'clock, time for you to telephone.' He passed the telephone to Maurice who dialled and waited. It was a full minute before it was answered. The voice on the other end was breathless as though its owner had been running. 'Venerable English College.'

'My name is Farther Lavoire, I was at the College this morning, visiting Bishop Horniev. I am just about to get on the train back home, but I thought I ought to ring you because the Bishop seemed very unwell when I left him. I mentioned it to the young man who let me out.'

'Yes, that was me, Father. It was fortunate you did tell me because the Bishop has suffered a collapse. The doctor is with him now.'

'I'm so sorry. Is the Bishop to be moved to hospital? I should like to keep in touch with his condition.'

'I don't know all the details… Here's the Rector, he will speak to you.' There was a pause, then an authoritative voice came on the telephone. 'Father Lavoire?'

'Yes Monsignor.'

'I'm sorry I missed you when you called. The Bishop seems to have had a heart attack. The doctor is still with him. I am afraid it is very serious. There is no question of moving him to hospital at present. I am just going to telephone … telephone one or two of his friends to let them know.'

Maurice, prompted by the slight hesitation in the Rector's voice, decided to take a chance. 'Could I come around? I will cancel my train and travel tomorrow.' Arthur, who had been a party to one side of the conversation only, made urgent signs. Maurice ignored him.

There was a slight, but significant, pause before the Rector spoke again. 'I shouldn't do that if I was you. We may be very busy here. By all means keep in touch by telephone.'

Maurice smiled with satisfaction. 'Yes, thank you, Monsignor. Again, I'm so sorry. I will remember him in my prayers. Give him my best wishes.'

'Thank you, Father, I will, goodbye.' As Maurice put down the telephone, Arthur started to speak. Maurice held up his hand. 'Before you start, he's collapsed and they are not moving him. I think they have notified the Pope.'

'Let's go.' Arthur was already on his way out of the apartment, grabbing his coat. Maurice and Rex followed. After the black Mercedes drove out of the garage, Lia positioned herself near the window for what might be a long vigil. Arthur drove the car purposefully, but at moderate speed, the other two sat in the back.

They made their way across the Ponte Garibaldi, along the Via Arenula, turning left into the Piazza Benedetto Cairou and straight on to the picturesque Via di Giubbonari, slowing to pass through the Campo de Fiore and across to the Via dei Pellegrino. Arthur slowed to a crawl and turned into a narrow street which joined the Via Monserrato. He pulled up almost opposite the English College, where he could see the comings and goings. Two cars were parked outside the College. They had not been in position for more than a minute when one of the double doors opened and a small fat man dressed in black, carrying a black bag, hurried to one of the cars and drove off, obviously the doctor.

***

Peter Dunne had scarcely decided that it was time for bed when the bell rang summoning him to the papal study. It was a most unusual occurrence. He looked at his watch. Leo should be in bed at this time. Perhaps he wanted to give Peter some instructions for first thing the next morning or he wanted Peter to do some private errand for him. He had been very silent and withdrawn during that morning's daily conference. Peter hurried to answer the summons, taking his coat as he went. One never knew what the Pope had in mind.

Spartov was dressed in black. His face was drawn and he looked very tired. He spoke without preamble. 'I have had distressing news. My old friend, Bishop Horniev, has been taken ill at the English College. He collapsed a short time ago and he is not expected to live. I must visit him immediately.' Spartov was beginning to detest the whole charade. He was unsure how long he could go on with his part. Peter was glad he had brought his coat.

They descended in the antiquated lift to the garage where Sarto was waiting for them with the black

Mercedes. Spartov gave brief instructions and got into the back of the car with Peter. The Mercedes murmured its way out of the garage and through the Santa Anna gateway into the Roman traffic which was still quite busy. A muffled young man, in the black Lancia parked opposite, made a note on his pad.

A short time later Maurice and Arthur both saw the car at the same time. It was impossible to see the passengers but Sarto was driving. Good, it made things much simpler. The car came to a halt immediately opposite the doors of the College. Someone in the building had evidently been watching because the doors were thrown open at the same instant. Arthur watched carefully. The nearside rear door of the car was opened from within and out stepped a middle-aged cleric quickly followed by the unmistakable figure of the Pope albeit dressed in black. They walked rapidly across the short piece of pavement and up steps into the darkened hallway. The doors slammed shut. There were few people about. Two men walking towards the car stopped momentarily, then carried on their way with curious glances at the unresponsive doors of the College. The only other human in the street was a young girl walking in the opposite direction. No one appeared to have recognised Pope Leo.

Sarto pulled away from the kerb and then turned into a street which led around the block. The car silently disappeared from view. 'Good, your information was correct,' said Arthur. 'We'll give them a few minutes and then we can take up our positions. Don't forget, make no move until you see someone give the driver the word.'

Arthur powered his own Mercedes in the direction taken by the papal car. They circled the block and saw it parked in a road leading off the Via Monserrato just around the corner from the College. He pulled into the kerb twenty metres behind and settled down to wait. The side street was deserted. Most of the city would be asleep at this time. Arthur cared little one way or the other. Success depended on surprise.

Two cats were chasing one another around a lamp post and a sheet of newspaper was blowing high in the air. The street was narrow but well kept, shutters newly painted and windows bright. After about half an hour, a young man dressed in black, priest or seminarian it was impossible to say, came around the corner at a trot, from the direction of the College. Maurice and Rex got out of the car and began strolling along the pavement. The black figure ran along, stepped off the pavement to the driver's side of the car where Sarto had the window fully lowered. He spoke a few words to Sarto and then quickly disappeared back the way he had come. Maurice breathed a sigh of relief. If the young man had stayed with the car it would have made things difficult. The plan was still going smoothly.

Sarto was starting the car. Maurice quickened his steps to a run while Rex moved out around the back of the car. Sarto, who already had his window lowered looked up startled as Maurice rapped on the opposite window. He waved his hand to indicate that he had pressing business. Maurice tapped again. Sarto, with a look of impatience, pressed a button and the electric powered window slid silently down. Sarto leaned over, resting his arm on the passenger seat, the other still gripping the steering wheel.

'Sorry, Maurice, I can't stop now, urgent...' That was as far as he got. With practised ease, Rex put his arm through the fully lowered window on the opposite side, felt for the control and wrenched the door open and, as Sarto half turned to see the cause of this new intrusion, he received the full force of the lead-weighed cosh in the middle of his forehead. He slumped over without a sound, his peaked chauffer's cap spinning off his head. Rex reached into the car with one gloved hand and switched off the ignition. Maurice reached through the window and grabbed the cap. He turned and walked quickly to their own black limousine which Arthur was edging slowly past. Maurice gave the peaked cap to Arthur and then opened the rear door and flung himself in. He heard Rex slam the door on Sarto and then he was with Maurice in the roomy interior, closing the door as the car picked up speed. Arthur touched the switch and the number plates changed as they turned the corner. Maurice positioned himself out of site behind the rear door pillar as they drew up outside the College. Rex sat in the opposite corner. For a few minutes nothing happened and Maurice felt a ball of tension obstructing his throat. He looked at Rex who sat, relaxed and vacant, in the opposite corner. Arthur was pretending to be occupied with something under the dashboard so that his face would be obscured.

Suddenly, the main College door opened and the middle-aged cleric they had seen before, walked out across the short pavement and Stretched out his hand towards the rear door. The Pope walked four or five paces behind so that he could get straight into the car without pausing.

Peter had not understood what had been said. Leo had spoken to Bishop Horniev in Czech. The old man was clearly dying and Leo was clearly too upset to administer the Sacrament of the Sick himself. The air in the street felt sharp and refreshing after the smell of death inside the English College. He could see that Sarto was fussing with something under the steering wheel. He smiled to himself as he opened the rear door and slightly bowed his head as Leo bent to enter the car. What happened then was confused and unreal. He was aware of the figures of the Rector and Vice-Rector standing discreetly back inside the hallway of the College. They made a sudden quick movement. At the same time, Leo literally shot into the dark interior of the car. Peter, who had been on the point of following, was momentarily paralysed, his hand still on the handle of the door. He was unprepared for the acceleration of the car which pulled him off his feet and slammed the door at the same time.

Spartov was sprawled full length on the floor of the car as it moved rapidly down the Via Monserrato. He started to rise. 'Stay right there, Holy Father, I have a gun pointed at your head.' Maurice had flopped down into his seat after his exertions and now cradled a small automatic in his hand. Sweat was sticking the thin cotton hood to his face. Spartov subsided onto the floor and gingerly touched his forehead. A large bump was already beginning to form. He wondered why he had not been shot and killed as he crossed the pavement. Presumably because they wanted him alive. Realisation dawned; his Soviet masters had heard what happened in the Synod and they had decided to remove him before he did more damage. They had not shot him because his body would have been examined and the secret of the substitution revealed in the minute scars of plastic surgery. He had little doubt that he was being taken to a place from where he could be moved to Russia without fuss, possibly to the Embassy.

Arthur drove at high speed past Michelangelo's towering Palazzo Farnese on the right, towards the

Theatre of Marcello, standing ruinous opposite the bridge of Cestio Farbricio. They were running alongside the Tiber now, heading almost due south and he pressed the switch which returned the number plates to their proper place. He continued to drive, less quickly now, down the Lungotevere Aventino until he reached the Pont Sublicio. He swung the car, amid a diminishing tide of smaller cars and scooters, and crossed into Trastevere, past the hospital di S Michele and headed directly for the apartment. He had taken a long way around to throw off any possible pursuit, but the plan had worked so perfectly that he doubted there would be any chance of being followed. Still, he did not believe in taking chances.

Lia had been watching for them and the heavy steel shutter rolled up as they cruised gently around the little piazza. Arthur did not relax until the engine was turned off and the shutter descended once more.

Rex, who had not moved throughout the whole operation, now climbed out of the car and, standing well out of sight, waited. Lia handed him the blindfold and he secured it over Spartov's head, leaning into the car to do so. When it was done, he and Maurice took off their hoods.

'Now get up and get out of the car,' said Maurice, prodding Spartov with the toe of his shoe.

***

Peter was kneeling, looking at the Roman pavement. He had just decided that it was just as dirty as pavement anywhere else when strong arms gripped him at either side and hauled him to his feet. He shook his head to get rid of the curious hazy feeling and looked from on to the other. 'Are you alright, Monsignor?' It was the Vice Rector who was speaking. He must have fallen. He looked from one to the other. They were worried about something. Memory, shutting out the unacceptable, finally succumbed.

'The Holy Father, what happened?' Peter addressed the Rector this time.

'We don't know Peter. Do you think your chauffer has had some kind of breakdown?' The Rector's face was grave. He was a stocky, grey haired English exile of middle age. Peter's head was clearing rapidly now. He felt the warm trickle of blood running down his cheek and the side of his head was beginning to throb. He began to walk unsteadily back to the College doorway, clasping a reddening handkerchief to his ear. The Rector and Vice Rector walked either side. Uncertainty reigned. At that moment Sarto appeared at the far corner of the block, leaning heavily on the stonework. The three clerics ran towards him, Peter forgetting his damaged ear. If Sarto was still there, who was driving the papal car? Sarto was barely coherent. Peter saw the car, still parked in the side street. They half carried Sarto and laid him in the back. The street was still deserted except for an old beggar who was shuffling along the other side of the street. 'Thank God most of the city is asleep,' said Peter fervently. 'Alex, 'He addressed the Vice Rector. 'Signor Sarto is in no condition to drive back to the Vatican and I'm still rather shaken. Will you drive us both?' Without waiting for an answer, he turned to the Rector. 'Telephone Cardinal Carelli, tell him what has happened and tell him to expect me. Don't notify the police yet. The Cardinal will know what to do.'

***

Spartov lay on the bed. The steel bracelet was secured around one wrist. The four stood some distance away. Arthur held an automatic levelled at Spartov's chest. He bowed stiffly. 'We regret to inconvenience you in this way, your Holiness.' His voice was muffled slightly by the hood. 'However, we will do everything within reason to make your stay comfortable. Hopefully, it will not be a long one. One of us will stay with you at all times. The hoods are for your protection as well as ours. If you should see and be able to identify any of us, we will be obliged to kill you to avoid future recognition. If you attempt to escape, we will shoot you. Do you understand and are you prepared to co-operate?'

Spartov suddenly understood. They were not Russian Agents but common criminals who had kidnapped him, presumably for ransom. As the full implications hit him, he began to laugh uncontrollably.

Arthur was puzzled. 'I don't think you quite see the position. If your Church does not satisfy our demands, you will be killed.'

Spartov recovered himself with difficulty. 'It is you who do not see the position. What you are doing is wrong but I sense that most of you are misguided rather than wicked. If you persist, death surely lies ahead for all of us. Release me and I will use my considerable influence to ensure that you are not traced by the police. I strongly urge you to listen to me for your own good.'

Something of the magnetism which Spartov had absorbed in his role was felt by the four hooded figures watching him. Maurice shifted uneasily and he sensed that it was as much as Lia could do to stop herself falling to her knees. Authur broke the spell.

'It's too late for that, we are already committed, we must go now. There are books on the floor by the bed.' He motioned Rex to stay as they left the room. He locked the door after them.

'Now for the ransom demand,' said Arthur when they were once more comfortably seated in the lounge and divested of the cotton masks. Maurice sat in an armchair wondering if it was really true that they had the spiritual leader of countless million Catholics safely locked away in the upstairs room.

Lia sat stiffly on the sofa, visibly white hands clasped around her knees to stop herself trembling. Only Arthur appeared unaffected by events, probably because he had lived with the idea for so long. He was obviously well pleased with himself as he poured out generous measures of grappa into three tumblers. 'You will remember that I warned you that the snatch was always the easiest part, but I think we can congratulate ourselves on the really professional way we have handled things so far. If things continue to go our way, we will be away from here very soon, with a fortune at our disposal. We will get in touch with the authorities in about an hour. Give them time to sweat a little first and make them more receptive to our requirements. Keep the radio on. When the news breaks we will have no difficulty in extracting the money. It will pour into Rome from Catholics in every country in the world.

***

Peter had intended to go straight to Cardinal Carelli's office and he asked the Vice-Rector to drop him there before proceeding to get assistance for Sarto. A young priest, however, whom Peter recognised vaguely as being from the Secretariat of State, stopped the car just inside the Porta Sant Anna and instructed them to drive directly to the small first aid station where their injuries were to receive attention. Only when he was declared sufficiently recovered did Carelli wish to see Peter and then he could attend upon him immediately.

Peter permitted himself to be examined, his scratches and bruise cleaned and a plaster applied. The brother who administered the treatment completed it by prescribing a tumbler of rough red wine, which was much appreciated. Sarto's injury was viewed with much concern and the doctor decided to move him to a local hospital for observation. The young priest gave Sarto strict instructions that he must say nothing except that he had been struck while out on an errand. Peter saw the young priest go with him as he departed in the ambulance.

Peter fretted with impatience. The Vatican was moving at its usual deliberate pace. He wondered what he had expected; everyone rushing around in a blind panic? What would it take to create blind panic in the Vatican? Peter could think of nothing. Even the last trumpet blast would be referred to the College of Cardinals for a decision.

At last the ministrations of the brother were at an end. Peter's ear still smarted but it was the antiseptic, rather than the bruise itself that was the irritant. After thanking the brother warmly for his attention and feeling faintly ridiculous with a great plaster clapped over one ear, he hurried to the Secretariat of State. Carelli's secretary directed him to the number three, smallest, conference room. Peter knocked on the cedarwood door and Carelli's unmistakable voice cried 'Entra Entra.'

He entered the room and found himself facing four men seated at a small table. Carelli motioned him to a seat. At the head of the table sat a wizened old man with an enormous hooked nose and thin, humourless lips. Peter recognised him instantly as Cardinal Bangio. The Camerlengo had already taken up the reins of the Church, presumably because it could not be known with certainty that the Pope still lived. On one side sat Archbishop Longini from the Holy Office. The fourth man was about fifty years old, very bald with a long solemn face and dressed completely in black. Peter did not recognise him. He bowed briefly. 'Your eminences, Your Grace,' and quickly sat down on Carelli's right and found himself facing the stony-faced man in black.

In answer to a question from Carelli Peter related all he knew about the incident outside the English College. Cardinal Bangio asked after Sarto and enquired whether Peter felt well enough to stay for the meeting. 'Your presence would be most valuable, Monsignor.' The voice was brittle and dry like fallen leaves before the dampness of winter completes the process of decay. The Camerlengo seemed genuinely concerned, however, and Peter read in his eyes the silent plea that all this nightmare could vanish and relieve him of the dreadful responsibility for the continued welfare and functioning of the Church. Peter made it quite clear that he would stay for the meeting and that he felt very well indeed, which was not quite true.

The Camerlengo nodded. Since his expression did not change, Peter was left to assume that he was pleased. The old man picked up a pencil and consulted a notepad which lay in front of him. The purple amethyst of his episcopal ring flashed as he tapped the pencil on the table. He looked up at Peter.

'For your benefit, I will recapitulate the situation as it now stands. Upon receipt of your message, His Eminence notified me. From the evidence at our disposal, it appears that the Holy Father has been taken away by unknown persons against his will. What their motives are we have yet to discover, but it seems unlikely that he is in immediate personal danger, since it would have been a simple matter to have murdered him as he approached the car, although we must assume the worst. For some reason the kidnappers, for such they are whatever their motives, wished to take him alive. Taking that into account and bearing in mind the traumatic effect the news of his abduction would create in the whole Christian world, I have taken the decision that, for the moment, we should not notify the Italian authorities and knowledge of the affair is confined to persons sitting around this table, one of the Cardinal's aides who has gone with Signor Sarto and, of course the Rector and Vice-Rector of the English College, who have been instructed to say nothing to anyone. We cannot keep the Holy Father's disappearance secret indefinitely, but I shall speak to his personal household staff, audiences and public appearances will be cancelled on the grounds that the doctor has ordered him to be confined to bed due to a feverish cold. We have all remonstrated with the Holy Father for his unfortunate habit of flitting around without warning or adequate safeguards.' He put down the pencil and clasped his hands, as though in prayer. 'I have summoned Fr Aretzi,' He nodded to the man in black. 'He is personal assistant to the Superior general of the Jesuits. We have not yet decided upon a course of positive action, but it is fitting that Fr Aretzi is here since the Jesuits owe a very special duty to the Pope.'

Peter's head was beginning to throb, partly due to his injury and partly as a reaction to the almost unbelievable situation in which he found himself. He felt as though he was looking at the scene from outside himself. He wondered what on earth, or in heaven, the five men grouped impotently around the table, could do. His mild attack of schizophrenia was interrupted by a discreet knock on the door.

A young priest entered. Peter recognised him as Carelli's secretary. 'I beg pardon for intruding,' he said. This envelope has been delivered to the Porta

Sant Anna a few moments ago. It appears urgent. I questioned the guard but he says that it was handed to him by a young street urchin who immediately ran away.'

Very good, Father, thank you.' Carelli laid the envelope in front of the Camerlengo. The outside bore the words: CARDINAL CARELLI, which had been cut out and pasted down, evidently from a magazine or newspaper. Another cut-out at the top of the envelope read: MOST URGENT.

The Camerlengo sighed audibly and ripped open the flap.

Should we not take care in case there are fingerprints?' suggested Peter.

The old man paused fractionally. 'I doubt that whoever took the trouble to cut out and paste letters on the front would overlook the possibility of fingerprints,' he said, extracting a sheet of paper from inside. The message, was in Italian and again composed of cut-out and pasted letters. The English translation was as follows:

THE POPE WILL BE RELEASED UNHARMED ON RECEIPT OF $100,000,000. INSTRUCTIONS WILL FOLLOW BY TELEPHONE TO CARDINAL CARELLI. YOUR AGREEMENT SHOULD BE NOTIFIED VIA VATICAN RADIO AT 1600 HOURS TOMORROW.

Carelli shook the envelope and out fell something which glinted and twinkled: the Fisherman's Ring, the personal ring made for each pope and broken up on his death. 'There is no doubt then that this message is from the people who took the Holy Father.' If it was possible, the Camerlengo looked even older. 'The Church would have to broadcast a world-wide appeal to obtain such a sum.' Carelli's eyes looked as if they were about to leap from their sockets.

'I think there can be no question of such an appeal.' The Camerlengo spoke quietly but with authority. 'However, the immediate problem is what do we do about the radio broadcast?'

Archbishop Longini spoke for the first time. 'I'm sure you are right Eminence. I think we should broadcast a message which can be taken to mean that we acquiesce. We need time more than anything at the moment.'

Carelli nodded vigorously. 'I agree, I agree.' The Camerlengo looked at Aretzi.

'Your Eminences, Your Grace, Monsignor.' Aretzi had a deep sonorous voice, which went perfectly with his physical appearance.

'May I suggest that, firstly, we continue to keep the matter confidential, secondly, Vatican Radio broadcast a message which I will draft for your approval and, finally, you leave the solving of this problem to our society which, as you have pointed out, has a special duty to the Holy Father. We have many talents within our organisation. Perhaps you would give me leave to recruit such members as are necessary. I will have a man here within the hour to oversee the switchboard and check any messages for Cardinal Carelli.'

The old man at the head of the table, the dry as dust old man sitting in his black and purple soutane like a small child in clothes a size too big, the shrunken figure demonstrated why he had been chosen to be Camerlengo of the Holy Roman Church. 'Please proceed as you suggest and keep Cardinal Carelli informed.' His decision was immediate and it was clearly final. The meeting broke up after a prayer for the safety of the Pope and another prayer for divine help and guidance in their task.

Peter came out of the Secretariat of State and stood in the courtyard of San Damaso. He took several deep breaths to clear his head. Father Aretzi had rushed away immediately and left the three prelates conversing in low voices. Peter decided to take a stroll around the garden. It was quite dark and it was cold, but he wanted to think and he needed to be alone. Brackets fixed here and there, seemingly at random, on the massive walls shed large enough pools of light to enable Peter to see where he was going. He walked through the old block of the Vatican towards the garden, through courts which conjured up, in their very names, the history which pervaded every stone: the Parrot Court, the Courtyard of the Borgia and the Court of the Sentry. A succession of dark tunnels opening up into scarcely less dark wells between high stone walls. Hardly any of it was planned in the accepted sense. The buildings simply jostled together, not in a comfortable homely way but as though they were fighting for power long gone. There was always something eerie about this part of the old city. Around each corner, he half expected to see a scene of Renaissance revelry suspended in time.

It was with a feeling of relief that he stepped out beyond the corner of the Sistine Chapel and passed the more modern power plant. He decided to walk through the formal gardens which lay beyond the Apostolic Library, as if the orderly layout of bushes, trees and plants could impose some sort of order into his mind. He had seen the day change from triumph to disaster. He remembered the spontaneous applause of the bishops the previous day and Leo's lack of enthusiasm. The Pontiff had been very much preoccupied during the morning, in spite of the obvious success of the Synod.

Now that the Pope was gone Peter realised, perhaps for the first time, the pressures which went with the high office. He was sure Leo was unwell and he knew that his doctor was very frustrated when he left him. Could the strain of leading the world's Catholics be too much? It had been too much for Pope

John Paul I. Leo had packed so much into such a short period of time. Peter had never believed in premonitions in the generally accepted sense, but for weeks he had had the feeling that something was about to happen. Some Popes were said to have presages of their own deaths; Pius XII for example. Could that have happened to Leo? He doubted it. He did not lay great store by such things. Pius XII had been 82 when he died. At that age anyone with a papal workload would not expect to live long. The Holy Spirit was supposed to guard the pope against teaching error. Why should that be relevant in the present circumstances? He decided that it wasn't relevant. There was something about the Pope which worried him but he could not yet put his finger on it.

What had caused Leo to become withdrawn and…sad, yes that was the word. Why was he so sad? Peter tried to think back to the time he first noticed it. It was difficult because Leo was nothing if not unpredictable. He stopped suddenly. He remembered Leo' face as he emerged from the private ward full of instruments clicking and clacking around the dying body of the gardener. Leo had become more and more wrapped up in himself from that moment. Perhaps it was just coincidence. Peter's mind went back to the old man's confession. With a great effort of will he banished it.

He decided to stop this train of thought which was getting him nowhere except along paths he did not wish to tread. He found that he had walked almost up to the Radio Station housed in the former Vatican Observatory. Before that the impressive masonry had housed one of the towers with which Leo IV had punctuated the walls originally built for the protection of the Vatican. Inside the building, the voice of the Pontiff would be being beamed, at that moment in different languages, to various parts of the world. All quite usual.

He retraced his steps, then cut through the dark Belvedere Court and into the village. He could see, in the distance, that the Swiss Guard had closed the gates on the outside world. He must have been walking for well over an hour. He nodded to one of the security guards stationed outside the rusticated arch and made his way to the telephone exchange. Another guard stood outside, chewing gum. He gave Peter the briefest of glances as he went inside. The Pope's private secretary was well known to them all.

Inside, Peter made his way to the main switchboard. A rota of nuns operated it. Five of them were on duty and one looked up, faintly startled. Visitors were infrequent. The long low switchboard was virtually silent except for the clicking of switches manipulated by nimble fingers and the low murmur of voices speaking in many tongues. He wondered how the nuns heard anything through the earphones clamped over their black veils. The Sister Supervisor put down her own headphones and came over to meet him with a smile.

'Good evening Monsignor, is there something I can do for you? We seem to be inundated with visitors. Is there some difficulty?' Her face was serene, she evidently suspected nothing of the drama of the day. Peter must be careful not to give her cause for alarm.

Good evening Sister. I believe there is a ...that is...Father...I forget his name.' Peter stopped aware that he was making a mess of things. He realised that he could not simply say 'Look here, can you tell me if the man who is to intercept calls from the Pope's kidnappers has arrived?' He gathered his wits and tried again. 'I believe someone is going to inspect the equipment. Maybe there is a fault of some kind?'

'Oh yes, Monsignor, so sorry. I am getting quite forgetful. It seems that calls to Cardinal Carelli are suffering from interference. The young man is just coming through here. I hope it's nothing serious. Sometimes I think the new equipment is scarcely an improvement. Workmanship isn't what it was don't you think?' She did not wait for, nor seem to expect, an answer as she bustled him through a glass panelled door at the end of the room, where a young, rosy cheeked priest sat at a desk with a tape recorder and a mass of meters and trailing wires. He wore headphones and a look of intense concentration as he adjusted a knob on the small console in front of him. He looked up enquiringly when Peter entered.

'Thank you, Sister, I may be some time.' Peter waited until the nun had bustled out and closed the door. 'I'm Peter Dunne, the Pope's private secretary. I was at the meeting with Father Aretzi. You must be Father …?' 'Acosto, Roberto Acosto.' The young priest smiled, revealing in the smile lines, which fell too easily into well-worn wrinkles that the initial impression of youth was somewhat flattering. Peter decided that he must be one of those people who looked forever young. 'You wasted no time in getting here. What are you hoping to do?' Peter waved at the mass of equipment. Acosto smiled.

'I was sent straight over. As a matter of fact, I am usually stationed here in the Radio Station and Father Aretzi came straight to me after the meeting. As to what I can do, that is very limited I'm afraid. That is the trouble with these modern switchboards, so much is automatic. I have linked up with the switchboards next door and arranged that any call to Cardinal Carelli is switched through here at the same time as it is switched through to his Eminence. I can record the call and make some attempt to trace it although my trace will be very rough. To mount a proper trace, we would have to call in the Roman Telephone authorities and I understand that that is out of the question at the moment. The trace is only possible at all because of these meters I have rigged up and the particular wiring combination of the boards next door. You see three of the boards are solely concerned with overseas calls and the remaining two deal with calls from inside the country.' Acosto paused. "Well it's all rather complicated but ...' He broke off suddenly and quickly switched on his recorder. Peter felt his heart beat faster as he watched the quietly efficient man at the table in front of him fiddle with the dials and adjust two large knobs in the centre of the console. After about a minute, he switched off the recorder and set it to rewind.

'What was it?'

'It was a call for the Cardinal but not the one we are expecting. I suppose that will not come until after the broadcast tomorrow. I just used this call as a dry run. I managed to trace it as coming from somewhere in north Italy. 'As a matter of fact, it was from the Archbishop of Milan but I don't expect our friends to identify themselves or their location so readily.'

'I will come back tomorrow, if I may, and sit in on the call with you.' Peter's heart was returning to its natural rhythm.

'Thank you, I shall be glad of the company. I will be relieved in about two hours and I come back on duty at noon tomorrow.'

23. THE SAFE HOUSE

Monday, 5th February 1979

Arthur sat in the armchair, Lia and Rex, as usual, on the sofa. Maurice was taking his turn with the prisoner in the room upstairs.

'It's a few minutes before four o'clock. Turn up the radio.' They were the first words Arthur had uttered for over an hour. Lia leaned forward and turned up the volume. The sound of the Sistine Choir flooded the room. 'Not so loud.' Lia obediently adjusted the control. The sound of the choir faded and the announcer informed listeners that they had indeed been listening to the Choir of the Sistine Chapel. After the chimes, broadcast directly from the basilica, the announcer reminded listeners that they were listening to Vatican Radio. Rex lounged back, his eyes staring dully at the small transistor radio. Lia's hand felt for his. She sat bolt upright on the edge of the seat. She noticed that small globules of sweat had formed on the bald dome of Arthur's head.

Before the next programme, here is an announcement.' Pause which seemed to stretch to eternity. 'The Secretary of State to the Holy See, Cardinal Carelli, today indicated his agreement to a proposal which will have far reaching effects upon the organisation of the Vatican State. His Eminence stated that he hopes to be in a position to finalise the matter later today.' The announcer sounded puzzled. 'The next programme...'

Arthur leaned forward and turned off the radio, a look of triumph accompanied the colour returning to his face. 'Pathetically easy, he is even inviting us to get in touch with him later today.'

'But there has been no news of the Popes kidnap, either in the papers or on the radio,' said Lia.

Arthur looked smug. 'Don't you see, the wording of the announcement we just heard clears up that little mystery for us. They are keeping the affair secret. That can only mean that they are confident of raising the money without an appeal.' He mused to himself for a moment. 'That cuts two ways of course. There is the temptation to think that we should have asked for more' but, on the other hand, if the affair is being kept secret, we should have little fear of discovery unless the Italian police have been told which, somehow, I doubt. The idea of being chased by a detachment of Swiss Guards with pikes at the ready is a little bizarre.' Clearly Arthur was in a good humour. He missed Maurice at that moment. He realised that he had come to rely on Maurice for sensible comments. Lia was alright and could be trusted to do her part, at least until the ransom was paid; after that he had his doubts. Rex, he had decided, was a dangerous psychopath. He regretted inviting him to take part in the venture but there was no way he could get rid of him just yet. He could not afford to do anything with might lead the authorities, by however tenuous a link, back to him. Lia would be upset too, he imagined, if anything happened to Rex. Rex, however, would have to be ditched after it was all over. In the meantime, he might still have his uses if it came to a fight. Arthur suppressed an inward shudder at the thought of more violence; violence that he did not control.

'You had better be on your way Lia.' Rex stirred. 'I'll go with her,' he said.

'No need for that, Rex. She is in no danger, no one suspects us.' He spoke slowly and clearly as one addressing a child. Rex looked stubborn for a moment then relaxed. Arthur turned to Lia again. 'Go to the other side of the city, change buses and telephone from a public 'phone box. Come back by a roundabout route and buy some bread or pastries on the way so that everything looks perfectly natural.' As Lia left, he turned to Rex. 'Go relieve Maurice, will you?'

Rex got up and sauntered to the door. 'That Pope guy gives me the willies. If he starts preaching at me again, I may just stick him.'

'You do and it will be the last thing you do,' Arthur did not hesitate to reveal his dislike. 'Our prisoner is both the source of our income and our insurance if the worst should happen. Leave your knife on the table.'

Rex took his knife from inside his shirt and held it between finger and thumb. Arthur stood up and the two men stood facing each other in silence. Suddenly, the knife flew from Rex's hand. It embedded itself in the polished top of the small table between them. Arthur's automatic had appeared again, as if by magic.

'Half a second separated you from death my friend,' said Arthur.

Rex laughed contemptuously, turned his back and went through the door. Arthur could hear his knuckles tapping on the wall as he walked down the corridor. He pocketed the gun and sat down. He pulled out the knife and laid it on the table. The sight of the deep scar on the expensive and delicately crafted wood made him want to weep. People like Rex were no better than animals, in fact, animals were far better. He noticed, with distaste, that Rex had not bothered to properly clean the blade of the knife and traces of blood still adhered to it at the junction with the handle. He went to wash his hands. When he returned, Maurice was sitting waiting for him.

'Well?'

'Everything as we hoped, Maurice. Lia has gone to telephone the Cardinal. Now we must get ready for the final stage – the transfer of the money. How is our prisoner, by the way?'

'He is quiet. He seems to be occupied in prayer most of the time. It will need more than prayer to get him out of this. Nothing less than hard cash in fact.'

'Quite so.' Arthur poured them both a glass of wine. 'Now there is something we should discuss while the others are out of the way. I had intended to transfer the money south and then across to Yugoslavia. From there it was to have been deposited in four numbered accounts in a Swiss bank. I have arranged separate routes out of the country for the rest of you and we were all to meet at a small hotel in London two weeks after the cash is delivered. The only risk would be mine, since I would have the money with me until I left Italy. I can handle that.'

'Just a minute.' Maurice looked puzzled. I detect, from your choice of words, that you have revised your plans.'

Arthur examined the marked surface of the table and explored the extent of the damage with his fingertips. 'Very acute. There is nowhere we can be sure of being safe unless we all appreciate the necessity of behaving calmly. There is no room for the mentally unstable. What are we going to do about Rex? When all this is over I mean.'

***

Peter also listened to the broadcast on Vatican Radio then, having finished his administrative duties for the day, he joined Fr Acosto in the telephone exchange.

Just after six o'clock a call came through. Acosto worked rapidly at his instruments. At length he took off his headphones and looked at Peter. 'I must phone Fr Aretzi.' He quickly dialled a number. 'Yes, Acosto here. It came from eastern Rome somewhere in the vicinity of the Piazza di Spagna. Yes, I will.' When he was seated again, he rewound the tape. 'Listen, this was the call.' He pressed the PLAY button.

'Carelli.' There was no mistaking Carelli's voice which Peter had heard many times on the telephone.

'Is that Cardinal Carelli?' This time a woman's voice, difficult to say what age, obviously Italian, obviously nervous.

'This is he.'

'We heard your announcement on the radio agreeing to our demands. Prepare the money in used notes of varying denominations and have it ready in four briefcases.' Was this the voice of a terrorist? Peter wondered. A cold feeling hit his stomach.

'In four briefcases did you say? Carelli was obviously stalling to give Acosto time to get some kind of fix on the caller.

'Four. The money should be ready by noon tomorrow.'

'That scarcely gives enough time to …'

'Tomorrow or you will all be meeting to elect a new pope.'

'Can I not appeal to you in the name of Our Lord J…'

'Enough. At noon the briefcases should be put in the unlocked boot of a small blue Fiat 126 with a full tank and parked outside the telephone booth in the Piazza Navona. One priest, unarmed, should be in attendance. We will telephone the booth at exactly twelve o clock with further instructions. Twenty-four hours after we take delivery of the money, we will release the Pope.'

But…' Click, the line went dead. Acosta leaned over and switched off the tape and at the same instant the telephone rang. Acosto picked it up, listened a moment then gave it to Peter.

'Hello Peter, Carelli here. Would you come up to number three conference room in an hour's time?'

24. FR ARETZI

When Peter presented himself at the conference room, Carelli and Aretzi were the only others present.

'Ah, come in Peter and sit down.' Carelli was beaming, though why that should be Peter could not imagine. 'Fr Aretzi will outline his idea to you.'

Peter looked expectantly at the solemn Jesuit who returned his gaze impassively for a moment leaning across the table earnestly.

'Monsignor Dunne, I have heard the telephone message from the kidnappers and I immediately referred the matter to one of my colleagues who is an expert in that kind of thing. Obviously, we have dispatched men to the vicinity of the call but we have no real hope of apprehending anyone. However, it appears very likely that the Pope is being held in Rome. We have almost two days to arrange things but it is essential to settle the way we will proceed.'

Peter found the man's voice had a hypnotic quality, deep and soothing. He was quite prepared to believe that the Jesuit could sort everything out. After a brief pause, Aretzi continued.

'I have already outlined my proposal to His Eminence and, subject of course to the agreement of Cardinal Baggio, he agrees. Firstly, we want you to drive the car carrying the ransom money. Do you accept? There may be some danger, but it is important that we have someone intelligent and who knows what is at stake.'

'Of course.'

'Good, the ransom will be no real problem. $100,000,000 is a great deal of money and it will take some time to count. We propose filling the cases with about a quarter of that amount, which we will obtain partly from the Treasury and partly from the Banco di Roma. Since dollars are specified, it is more than we can supply from our own resources. We anticipate that the kidnappers will merely glance at the contents and leave the actual counting until they reach their hideout. I defy anyone to spot the discrepancy by glancing at the cases. If all goes well, we should be able to see the business through to a conclusion before they have started to count.'

'But I don't see how...'

'You will, all in good time. Do not forget that our Society has almost infinite resources of manpower and expertise. Your part will be simply to obey any instructions you receive.'

***

Five bull-necks sat in the KGB offices in Moscow. Five worried brows concealed similar emotions. The papal venture had started well but things seemed to be going wrong. Now the Ambassador had notified them that the gardener link man had been identified and shot. It appeared, however, that he had died without revealing anything although no one could be sure. Then there was the Synod. Rumours were abroad that it had gone well. But 'gone well' for the Vatican was bad for Russia. There had been no official word from the Vatican. What was Spartov doing? Was it time to terminate this particular experiment? They all felt very nervous. At length, the senior bull-neck spoke.

'I propose that the decision whether to terminate the venture should depend upon the statement from Spartov incorporating the decisions of the Synod. If the statement is not to our liking, Spartov will be judged to have failed and, therefore, he is not the man for this job. Arrangements for termination will be handled from our Embassy.'

They were all aware of the dangers involved, but there seemed to be nothing else to be done. The meeting signalled its agreement.

***

Carelli sighed. Dealing with a kidnapping was not what he expected when he was made Secretary of State. Fr Aretzi assured him everything was going according to plan, but he was worried. Arrangements for collecting the dollars from the Treasury and the Bank were well advanced and the following day would see the end of the affair, if all did indeed go well. But explaining the cancellation of papal audiences had led to speculation among the world's Press regarding the Pope's state of health. It was not helped by indiscreet remarks about the fragile nature of his health made by Professor Formenti to a group of American reporters. On top of everything else, the Russian Ambassador had been positively rude at a meeting that morning, demanding to see the Pope as a right. Life, Carelli ruminated, could be exceedingly complicated at times.

25. PAY DAY

Tuesday, 6th February 1979.

Arthur was in a good mood, thought Maurice, as he listened to him whistling tunefully in the bathroom.

This was the day. By evening they would be away from the city. He was rather sorry to leave Rome but not sorry to see the last of Rex. He had become more and more introverted as the weeks passed. Only Lia seemed able to manage him. They had managed very well the previous night if the noises reaching him through the thin partition had been any guide. It had been Arthur's turn to stay with the prisoner and Rex was supposed to be sleeping in the lounge; but at midnight, he had heard Lia's door open and close and, shortly afterwards, sounds of passion, not unrequited either, had permeated through to his room. No wonder they both had dark circles under their eyes.

Arthur interrupted his thoughts by breezing into the room with Rex. Lia was taking her turn upstairs.

'Sit down, Rex,' Arthur said, taking a seat himself. Rex obeyed yawning listlessly. 'Now today we make our fortunes. Lia will stay with the prisoner. I will operate the telephone from here. Maurice, you collect the hire car at eleven o'clock and be in position at twelve. Rex, you get in your place at the same time. You know what you are to do?'

'Yes.' Rex's tone was that of a spoilt child dealing with a fussy mother.

'Good, now let's all have a good breakfast and we will be fortified for the day ahead. I can't stand those stingy continental affairs – sorry Maurice.' Arthur giggled. Nothing was going to spoil his day anyway, he knew something about Rex that Rex did not know. Rex would not be around very long after the job was finished. He looked at Rex's expressionless face and giggled again.

***

Pietro Thomaso stood in front of Mangini's desk, waiting for the outburst. He had handed in his report the evening before and he knew he must have done something wrong when Mangini sent for him. Surprisingly enough, his superior did not look annoyed that morning, only slightly baffled.

'Pietro, you submitted a report three days ago.'

Three days ago! Thomaso shuddered. How could he remember what he had put down on his report three days ago? Those reports filled several A4 pages every day, logging down the comings and goings of various prelates and anyone else he recognised. When he had received his transfer to the special corps of Public Security, as a result of finding the first seed merchant's message, he assumed that it would be a world of thrills, but the only excitement consisted of visits to his superior's office to account for himself and that was the sort of excitement he could do without. Mangini appeared not to notice the signs of imminent asphyxia on Thomaso's face as he struggled to say something appropriate.

'You said something very interesting in your comments. You reported a black Mercedes, bearing the registration letters SCV1, leaving the Vatican at twenty minutes past one o'clock in the early morning. You noted the driver as being Signor Sarto, the papal chauffer, and you state that two figures in clerical black were in the rear of the car.' Mangini had Thomaso's report in front of him and he was struggling to decipher the typing.

'You could not identify the figures properly because the rear windows had tinted glass and your observation was made with difficulty through the driver's window, which he had open. However, you think the Pope was one of the two men. How sure are you of that?' Thomaso tried to recall the scene in his mind's eye. 'Not absolutely sure – but it did seem like it.'

Mangini grunted. 'Later that same day, you reported the same car driving at high speed into the Vatican with an unknown cleric driving. You saw the car stop just inside the gates and an urgent conversation taking place. Later an ambulance transported Signor Sarto to hospital. All very strange. There have been no reports of the Pope visiting anyone in Rome, but we hear that the Pope is unwell. Does anything strike you as odd about all this, Thomaso?'

Thomaso brought the whole of his limited intelligence to bear on the problem. 'Perhaps the Pope and Senor Sarto became ill at the same time. Hence the hurried drive back and Senior Sarto's visit to hospital.'

'But what if I tell you that I have made subtle enquires at the hospital and it transpires that Signor Sarto is suffering from concussion caused by a heavy blow on the head?' Mangini leaned back with a look of triumph at having totally confused the stupid oaf in front of him. Thomaso stood, saying nothing because he could think of nothing to say. He wished he was somewhere else. His wish was fulfilled because Mangini dismissed him.

Something very strange was afoot. Mangini's instincts told him so. He could not make the connection between the secret messages and the injury to Sarto, but he felt sure there was a link somewhere. Had the time come to telephone Pietro Liego, the Chief of Security at the Vatican? No, he decided, he must get a few answers first. Perhaps the Pope's private secretary was the key. It must have been the secretary in the car with the Pope, if it had been the Pope. Mangini sighed heavily and picked up the telephone. He directed a car to be on permanent standby to follow either of the two private secretaries, if they emerged.

***

Spartov had plenty of time to think. He recalled his military training. Problem: he was being held prisoner in a locked room somewhere, he did not know where, in Rome. His wrist was secured by a strong chain and he could not reach the door or windows.

He was watched constantly but his watchers were always unarmed or, at least, they showed no evidence of guns. The guards always kept out of range. He had decided that there were no more than four of them. One was watching him now. It was difficult to tell what she was thinking because she was wearing a hood. That was the problem and the assessment. There appeared to be no weak points.

At first, he had thought that the woman might be persuaded to release him but, quite apart from the fact that she admitted that she did not have a key, she was basically hard. The leader was equally hard although unfailingly courteous. Of the two other men, one was French, affable but quite immovable, the other was clearly mentally unstable. Spartov decided that he should reserve his energies for the unstable one. It was already obvious that he allowed himself to be unsettled too easily. Spartov would preach at him at every opportunity. If he could draw him near, he thought he had a good chance of overpowering him. After that he would have to play his hand as it came

***

Peter Dunne pulled up at the call box in the Piazza Navona. He looked at his watch; he was five minutes early. The contents of the car boot made him uneasy. He had never been near so much money in his life. He felt as if he should keep checking to make sure it was still there.

He looked about. The square, he corrected that description in his mind because it was too long and narrow to be called a square, was full of bustle. Old men with moustaches and scrubby chins, priests in black hats, women with shopping baskets and a sprinkling of tourists loaded with cameras and guide books formed a kaleidoscope around him. It was too early for the tourist season proper although the weather was very mild that day. The sun shone and danced on the waters of Bernini's fountain. What on earth could Father Aretzi do? Peter turned around to see if he had been followed. It was impossible to tell. There were a number of cars parked but he had no way of knowing whether one of them was following him. Perhaps he should have checked, although Father Aretzi had told him to behave quite naturally.

He thoughts were interrupted by the ringing of the telephone bell in the call box. He almost ran to answer it.

'Who is that?' It was a man's voice, oddly quiet and soothing. He spoke Italian badly, with an accent. If only, Peter thought, I was Italian, I would be able to recognise it.

'Peter Dunne, private secretary to His Holiness.'

'Good, listen. Go to the call box, number three, Central Railway Station. Wait for further instructions. You have fifteen minutes.' The telephone went dead. Fifteen minutes! He would never do it.

He arrived at the call box with just two minutes to spare. There was a delay because it was occupied. Peter fretted as he walked up and down outside the ranks of telephones. He had visions of his car being gone when he got out. At last, the voluble Italian matron emerged from the box and Peter darted inside. The telephone rang immediately. The conversation was repeated, but this time he was directed to the Via Venito. Peter ran out of the Station, unlocked the car and drove off. The black Lancia, of the Pubblica Sicurezza pulled out and followed.

From his position on the marble seat outside the Station, Rex watched then walked into the Station himself and rang the flat; after that, he took a taxi to another part of the city.

At the next stop, the mystery voice told Peter that he was being followed. 'Lose them or we will lose one prisoner.' Peter was in a panic. He had no experience of 'losing' a car. He looked over to where the black Lancia was parked. The man inside was reading a paper. The man on the telephone had given him a description of the car, even the registration number. Peter found it hard to believe that the middle-aged, balding man in the car was following him. But he could not afford to take chances, Aretzi had tried and, now, failed. He walked over to the Lancia and tapped on the glass. The man wound down the window, visibly shaken and on his guard.

'You've been seen. I have to lose you.' Peter turned back, got into the little blue Fiat and moved off.

***

Mangini received the news with a mixture of incredulity and rage. He noted the registration number of the little Fiat and slammed down the telephone only to pick it up again to detail two more cars to find the blue Fiat and report back.

What the hell was going on? Something important by the sound of it, but what? How did the Pope's secretary know he was being followed? 'You've been seen.' He pondered the words calmly. They could only mean that someone other than Monsignor Dunne had seen them. Could Monsignor Dunne be telephoning messages now? If so, would he be so foolish as to approach the security police direct? What was he doing, going from telephone to telephone? It was like one of those American movies he used to enjoy watching. He lost his cool and beat his head in frustration.

***

Peter was beginning to get very tired. He had lost the car or, more likely, it had lost him. That meant, presumably, that Father Aretzi was now out of touch, which meant, in turn, that it was all up to him. He felt hopelessly inadequate. He pulled up outside the seventh or was it the eighth call box. He realised that he was not far from the Beda College, to the south of Rome and outside the old city walls. He had two minutes to spare. The district was full of decaying blocks of so-called modern flats, washing hanging limply from their balconies like so much sad Christmas bunting. No one was about except an old man shuffling his way along the pavement. There was another blue Fiat parked just in front of him. The telephone rang.

'Leave your keys in the car and take the blue Fiat which you will see parked immediately outside this call box. Drive straight back to the Vatican. Do not stop. You will be watched.'

Peter came out of the box trembling. There was nothing he could do. If he disobeyed the voice, that might be the end of the Pope. But, if he obeyed, the kidnappers would be certain to discover the shortage of money as soon as they counted it. What could he do? He looked along the street again. Except for the old man, it was still deserted. Should he try and give a message to the old beggar? What could he tell him to do? He decided against it. So much for Father Aretzi. The kidnappers could not be far away because a car left with keys in the ignition in a district like this would be gone in ten minutes. In books and films, he thought, the hero would have a stunningly clever way of getting out of the mess. Then he laughed out loud as he realised he was casting himself as a hero and he had never felt less like a hero in his entire life.

Finally, he got into the car in front and drove away back to the Vatican.

***

It was dark. Lights were on all over the city. From his seat near the window, Arthur could not see any of the seven hills. He looked at his watch. Nearly five o'clock. It was half an hour since his last message to the Pope's secretary. Maurice and Rex should be back at five. Then he saw the blue Fiat moving slowly around the other side of the square and he was out of his chair in a moment and sprinting to the door. He clattered down the steps and operated the switch on the shutter. As it finished rolling into the drum, the Fiat inched gently into the garage and pulled up tightly behind the Mercedes. Arthur set the motor into reverse and, as the shutter rolled down again, Maurice and Rex jumped out.

'Any troubles?' asked Arthur.

'Not a scrap,' said Maurice, pulling off the grey wig and moustache. 'There was just one moment when he came out of the telephone box. I thought he must realise who I was. After all, I was the only person around; but then, like the postman and stray cats, beggars in Rome go unnoticed. He drove off. I got in the car, after checking that the cases were in the boot and full of money, then I picked up Rex, as arranged, and here we are.'

Rex was busying himself at the rear of the car, hauling cases out and setting them on the garage floor. 'Damn, they're heavy.'

'Sure you didn't ask for the cash in gold bars?' asked Maurice.

Arthur smiled complacently. 'Let's get them upstairs.' He turned and went up the steps, leaving Maurice and Rex to carry the cases, Inside the lounge, they saw that he had drawn the dining table into the middle of the room.

'Put the cases on the table,' he said. 'Rex, you go up and relieve Lia, she will probably be quicker at counting than you and she's been up there all afternoon.'

Rex looked truculent. 'Does it matter now,' he said. 'Anyway, how do I know that you will still be here when I come down,' Arthur fixed him with his cold eyes. 'It matters because we want to make sure that all the money is here. It will take a couple of hours to count it properly. You can come down and check your share when we have finished. We won't leave you behind because you must get it into your head that it is in all our interests that we are all happy and leave the whole business neat and tidy. If we left you, we would only be endangering ourselves.'

Rex looked sullen but he went. The logic seemed inescapable. Shortly afterwards, Lia came in. Maurice and Arthur had tipped the contents of the briefcases onto the table in readiness and her eyes bulged when she saw the notes.

'What do you think of that?' asked Maurice.

'Beautiful, just beautiful,' said Lia, eyes shining and lips moist. 'But wasn't it all too easy?'

'Not at all. I selected a victim with great care. I knew there would be no argument about the ransom. The Roman Catholic Church could not afford to lose its leader in this way. The fact that they have kept the whole affair out of the media bears out that they want to get the whole thing over with as soon as possible, suits me too.' Arthur laughed at his own cunning. 'Now, sit down and help us count. Count it into piles of half a million dollars and secure each half million with one of these.' He produced a packet of large elastic bands. 'It will then be easy to divide the money into proper shares.'

'It's not going to be easy. The denominations are all mixed up.' Said Maurice.

Don't worry, Maurice, I have never complained about counting money,' said Arthur.

They each drew a pile of notes towards them and began counting. Maurice noted that Lia's hands were trembling. Arthur was ice cool. It was clearly no surprise to him that everything had proceeded so successfully. All was silent, except for the rustling of notes and the muttering of figures in three languages. All was quiet for about half an hour.

Arthur was first to hear the bump. 'What was that?'

'It came from upstairs,' said Maurice.

'Damn him,' said Arthur. 'Carry on. I'll see what the trouble is.' He grabbed his hood and ran through the doorway. They heard him mount the stairs, two at a time. Maurice looked at Lia. Her face had gone white under her tan. She made no move to continue counting. At that moment, the bell rang from the street door.

Maurice was over by the window in an instant, but he could see nothing. 'Go and send them away, whoever they are,' he said. You are Italian, it will look better.'

Lia went, looking unhappy. He stood behind the door at the top of the stairs, listening. He heard sounds of revelry below and several vinous Italian voices raised in song. He smiled. The Italians were either roaring with rage or delirious with pleasure, there was no middle way. He closed the door and went back to the table to continue counting.

Arthur fumbled with the key. Sounds of scuffling came from inside the room. At last the key went home and the wards clicked. He flung the door open, gun ready. Spartov was half out of bed, blood oozing from a wound in his chest. Rex, his eyes filled with death lust, had drawn back his hand ready for a second plunge of the knife. He looked up at Arthur. 'I'll fix this bastard,' he said.

'No!' screamed Arthur, but the knife was already on its way. Spartov had taken the opportunity to roll off the bed and the knife buried itself into the mattress. Rex pulled it out and turned to finish his victim who was crawling away on the floor, but restricted by the chain. At that point, Arthur shot Rex neatly in the back of his head. The impact of the shot flung Rex face down across the bed, the knife still gripped in his hand.

Spartov had collapsed and seemed to be unconscious. Rex was clearly dead. 'What a bloody mess,' said Arthur aloud. It was true, in every sense.

Maurice half rose when he heard the shot. The door at the top of the garage steps opened and Lia walked through.

'Who was it?'

In answer, two men in dark suits and hats, muffled up to the eyes, followed her into the room. Both had guns and one was pointing at Maurice's chest.

'Sit down,' said the man with the gun trained on Maurice. His voice was hard.' Both of you keep quiet. Where is your prisoner and how many more of you are there?'

Maurice sat down again and Lia literally collapsed onto the sofa. 'He's upstairs,' said Maurice. There are two more with him.' Four more men, identically dressed, arrived from the garage. The man who appeared to be the leader waved his gun towards the door.

'Go through there and call them down, say it's urgent.'

Maurice did not argue, he had the nasty feeling that the game was up. When he got into the passage with the hard-voiced man close behind, he saw that the door to the stairs leading to the second-floor room was open. He stopped in the middle of the passage and shouted up as instructed. He heard the door slam and lock and Arthur coming down the stairs. He moved back to the hard-voiced man, who had been joined by two others.

There was a moment of silence, which seemed like an eternity, then Arthur appeared in the doorway, sweat making the hood cling to his cheeks. His reactions were quick. The automatic barked twice and the hard-voiced man and one of his companions reeled back, half turning towards each other in a deadly ballet, each firing an aimless shot as they fell. The third man had darted back into the lounge. Maurice stood rigid for a moment, then his legs turned to jelly and he slid down the wall in a dead faint.

Arthur stood indecisively. There was a fortune in the lounge but every instinct told him that it was now out of his reach. There was nothing else for it, he would have to secure his escape and start again. He fired at Maurice's limp body. It jerked once and resumed its former position, slumped against the wall like a rag doll. One less to inform on him. He would have to leave Lia. Pity, not very tidy. Arthur liked to retreat neatly. He was confident they would not trace him. He had a selection of passports and Arthur Brown was not, after all, his real name. He had always been careful.

He backed to the far end of the passage, feeling for the hidden catch with his right hand, covering the corridor with the automatic in his left.

He had barely touched the panel when it exploded in a mass of orange flame. It flung Arthur's limp body towards the far wall with the corpses of the two dead men. Arthur disintegrated and plastered himself indiscriminately over floor, walls and ceiling. The corridor filled with smoke, flames began to lick around the hole that had been the secret escape door. Three of the men in black raced out of the lounge, choking and gasping in the fumes, sliding on the floor, liberally strewn with pieces of splintered wood, plaster, torn clothes, blood and Arthur.

The blast had shattered the window under which the bodies lay. More men poured up the stairs and into the corridor through the secret panel. Three went straight up the stairs and fired the lock off the door. There was a slight delay while one of the men ran down to find out from Lia the whereabouts of the key to the steel handcuff.

She was in a state of collapse and they had to slap her hard and then administer brandy to get any sense out of her. She said that Arthur had the key in his pocket. Faced with the impossibility of finding the key among the mess that had been Arthur in the corridor, they shot through the steel chain and left the handcuff until later. Spartov was lifted onto the bed from which Rex was unceremoniously tipped onto the floor.

A small but voluble crowd, mainly from the trattoria across the piazza, had started to assemble outside. No one showed any inclination to enter the building, especially as the entrance was guarded by a large man with a gun prominently on display.

Inside, the men worked quickly. They searched the apartment thoroughly. They turned the two bedrooms into a shambles, looking for any evidence that could link the apartment to the Pope. Two men wrecked the kitchen and examined the insides of all cupboards and under each drawer. The desk in the lounge was locked and had to be smashed open. The contents were bundled into a briefcase. Lia collapsed again at this stage and she was carried out to one of the waiting cars.

Arthur's notebook and key were retrieved from the corridor and the handcuff was finally unlocked.

One of the men systematically sprinkled paraffin from a large can throughout the first-floor bedrooms and lounge and then descended to the garage and emptied the rest of the can over the concrete floor ready to be ignited as they left. He looked at his watch with a worried frown.

One of the men was evidently a doctor and pronounced Spartov alive but very ill. Maurice had been killed by the blast. A stretcher materialised and Spartov was taken down to a waiting ambulance. The two dead men in black were bundled onto more stretchers and taken away.

The man left in the lounge had replaced the notes in the cases and, within minutes, they roared away in five cars and two ambulances, leaving a hysterical Italian Crowd and a slightly smoking apartment behind. On leaving the piazza the cars split up and cruised off in different directions. One ambulance, siren wailing and lights flashing, screeched off at high speed.

With impeccable mistiming, Renaldo Mangini and a small force of the Publica Sicurezza arrived five minutes after the last car had left. Several varieties of Italian police followed hard on their heels. Flames were coming from the first-floor apartment.

***

Peter felt physically sick. He was sitting with Carelli in the latter's opulent office. He had made his report on the afternoon's happenings and now he felt drained. Not even the excellent red wine with which Carelli plied him seemed to make any impression. The Cardinal was unusually subdued.

They had been sitting there, lost in their own thoughts for almost an hour, when the telephone rang. Carelli listened for a few moments before turning to Peter. 'It's over. His Holiness is badly hurt and they are taking him directly to his private apartment. He has refused to go to hospital. Professor Formenti and His Holiness's confessor have been summoned.'

***

Spartov was propped up in bed. Formenti and the confessor had left. Carelli and Peter were alone with him. His breath came in a rattling wheeze and he had a bruise on his forehead. In the great basilica, Cardinal Bangio was preparing to celebrate Mass for the Pope's recovery. Ninety-six other cardinals and thousands of ordinary Roman citizens were in attendance.

Professor Formenti's prognosis had not been good. The world's press had been informed that the Pope was gravely ill.

'Give me the document, Monsignor.'

Peter handed over the closely typed sheets which Spartov had demanded be brought from his study.

'Pen?'

Peter passed the pen into the Pontiff's trembling hand. Spartov signed the document and lay back exhausted after the effort. He was fast losing consciousness.

'Peter.'

'Yes, Holy Father.'

'Release this immediately. It is the result of the Synod. It will probably be the last act of my Pontificate.'

Peter took the paper, hardly able to see for the curious wetness around his eyes. He bowed and hurried from the room.

26. AFTERMATH

Wednesday, 7th February 1979.

Four bull-necks sat around the table. The fifth had taken cyanide when the news broke. The summary of the conclusions of the Synod, proclaimed by the Pope, had shaken the world by its simplicity. The unity of all Christians to be put into practical effect within months, the theology to be ironed out over a period of ten years. This reversal of the usual procedure had brought cries of approval from all church leaders.

'Are we agreed, gentlemen?' The others gloomily nodded assent. 'Then I will notify the Ambassador to terminate the experiment. I have no doubt that Spartov is feigning illness at the moment to avoid the fate he must surely know awaits him. The termination must be made to look like an accident. We don't want a martyr. I will also set things in motion to get the Synod conclusions revoked.

The four men separated. They were under no misapprehension of what failure on such a project would mean. One shot himself soon afterwards, another resigned, a third was removed to an unpleasant posting elsewhere. By supreme irony, the fourth was eventually to go to a high position in the Praesidium.

***

'Father Aretzi, Your Eminence.'

Carelli rose to greet the sombre figure who followed the Cardinal's secretary into his office. 'Father, how are you? Please sit down. I have asked Monsignor Dunne to be present so that he can hear the details at first hand.' Carelli was his own flamboyant self, like a man with a weight suddenly lifted from his shoulders, which, in fact, he was.

Peter smiled. It hurt to smile he discovered, after a night without sleep. He had been all night at the Pope's bedside, together with a nursing sister. His head ached and he badly needed to rest, but he was determined not to miss this meeting and he had deputed all duties to the second private secretary until further notice.

Father Aretzi sat down. 'How is His Holiness this morning?'

Carelli became solemn. 'It is too early to say, according to Professor Formenti, but he seemed a little easier when I called this morning.'

'Good. I thank God.'

'Please now tell us what happened?' said Carelli.

'Yes, how did you pick up the trail after I warned your man off?' Asked Peter.

Father Aretzi looked puzzled. 'I had no report that you warned any of our men.' It was Peter's turn to be puzzled. Aretzi smiled for the first time, perhaps the only time for all Peter knew.

'My colleagues, however, did report that you approached a car bearing a representative of the Pubblica Sicurezza. What you said to him, I don't know, but you performed a valuable, notwithstanding an unwitting, service since he stopped following you at that point.'

Peter's jaw gaped open. He closed it. 'I give in, please explain and I will not interrupt.'

'Thankyou. First of all, let me make one little point. A policeman will always look like a policeman, in or out of uniform. People notice them. Who is not noticed, in Rome of all places?' He answered his own question. 'A priest. Or, in this instance, many priests. My expert on these matters immediately recognised the technique which would be employed as soon as it was known that you had to report to a telephone call box. It is a much-used technique, I understand, because the ransom money can be moved from place to place with no real possibility of being followed. The second part of the technique is to have a ransom car watched by one or more of the kidnappers, sometimes even the one who is doing the telephoning.'

'That accounts for the message I got to lose my tail,' said Peter.

'Precisely. As I was saying. My colleague recognised the technique and we planned accordingly. We have, you understand, many priests under out control in Rome itself and we brought in more for the occasion. Every call box in Rome and within a four-mile radius was watched by one of our priests.'

'Incredible!' exclaimed Carelli, unable to contain himself.

Aretzi smiled again. 'I will not go into the details. Suffice to say that your position was notified to our office within seconds of your departure from a call box by the simple expedient of telephoning from the same call box. Where the box was in a crowded place, our man could freely mingle with the crowd. Where the box was isolated, he had to conceal himself rather more carefully.'

'But what about the last stop when I was to leave the money and drive away?'

'We had a man in the block of flats opposite, sitting with a sick child. You gave him a few moments of anxiety when it appeared you might do something foolish. Fortunately, you changed your mind and when he saw you drive off and the old beggar take your car...'

'The old beggar, so that ...'

'Yes, another semi-invisible species I'm afraid. Anyway, our man immediately telephoned, telling us the direction in which the car was travelling.'

'But surely, you could not follow progress on foot no matter how many men you had.'

'Yes and no. Don't forget that each of our men knew the car number, make and colour. Its progress was pretty well charted by telephone to our central control. In addition, we had a number of cars in radio contact which we moved in a rough semicircle around your position. When your car was taken, it was a matter, literally of minutes until one of our cars established contact and could follow at a discreet distance. The rest was straightforward.

Two of our men were unfortunately killed and three of the four kidnappers. His Holiness was attacked, apparently one of the kidnappers was a very unstable character. The surviving kidnapper, a woman, is telling us the whole story.'

'What will happen to her?' asked Peter.

'That is a difficult question. It may be possible simply to release her. Apparently, she is very worried about the reactions of former Mafia friends to some of her activities and she shows very little desire to be released at present.'

'Was it absolutely necessary to kill the other three?'

'In a way they killed themselves. An Englishman, they called Arthur, who seems to have been the leader, seems to have shot the man who stabbed His Holiness. Then he tried to escape, having killed two of our men, through a secret panel leading to a sort of internal fire escape. Unfortunately for him, some of our men had decided to enter the apartment by the back entry. They could not open the panel from the outside so they prepared an explosive charge to blast their way inside. As soon as they heard shots from within, they detonated the explosive. He must have been right behind the panel at the time. He and his accomplice were caught in the blast. The motive for the kidnapping was purely monetary gain, no terrorist activity was involved.

'What about the police?'

'That's the strange thing. Our men got away minutes before both the police and the Pubblica Sicurezza arrived. It was to be expected that the police would turn up following the shots and the explosion. The Pubblica Sicurezza is another matter. It may be that you alerted them when you inadvertently approached one of their cars. But I think there is more to it than that. They were obviously following you. However, I cannot see how they can have known about the abduction of the Pope. Have they contacted the Vatican Security Staff do you think?'

Carelli did not know, but it was the work of a moment to find out. He replaced the telephone with a negative answer.

'Just a moment, said Peter. There was a detective at the hospital the night we went to see the old gardener. He was very anxious to find out something from him. Unfortunately, the old man died before he could be questioned,'

Aretzi looked thoughtful and tapped the table with surprisingly blunt fingers. 'Perhaps the time has come for a little judicious questioning. Should we not invite a representative of the Pubblica Sicurezza to see us and explain their interest in the gardener?'

***

It was the first time Mangini had been in the Vatican. He had been in St Peters of course, but this was rather different. He had been asked to an 'informal chat'. He progressed through what appeared to be miles of corridor and ante-room after ante-room before he finally arrived at the tiny office designated for his meeting with Father Aretzi. He knew of Father Aretzi. He was a hard man. Mangini could hardly refuse to attend. It could not be kicked upstairs as it would have been if, for example, the meeting had been official and with some higher prelate. The Vatican was, after all, an independent state. Aretzi was alone and Welcomed him cooly.

'Captain Mangini, several events over the past few weeks have suggested to us that your officers may be taking an unusual and possibly illegal interest in the citizens of the Vatican City State. There was the shooting incident, during which Signor Esseppi was fatally wounded, your attempts to question him and, most curious of all, perhaps, your agents' attempt to follow Monsignor Dunne, private secretary to His

Holiness. Your department has not had the courtesy to inform us of the nature of your investigation. Would you care to do so now, on an informal basis?'

Mangini played with his fingers, rapidly reviewing possible lines of approach to this unexpectedly direct question. His evidence had always been slim, moreover, he could hardly admit to prying into the affairs of the Vatican without having consulted with them first. He was aware that he had walked into a trap. There was nothing for it, he would have to deny any involvement in Vatican affairs.

'The shooting of Esseppi was most unfortunate, Father, the seed merchant was suspected of certain activities and we were anxious to question Esseppi because we were aware that he was a friend of his. I am not at liberty to divulge the nature of our investigations.'

'But I assume that you are assuring me that they had nothing to do with the Vatican, such an investigation would be a gross breach of our sovereign rights?'

The trap had closed and Mangini was committed. 'I am happy to give you that assurance.'

'Good. In that case, Captain Mangini, why were you following Monsignor Dunne?'

'Purely an error, Father, no more than that. The responsible agents have been severely reprimanded.'

'So, as far as the Holy See is concerned, there is and will be, no interest on your part?'

Mangini felt totally helpless. He knew that he was virtually closing the file. 'Quite correct. It would be unthinkable to interfere with your own excellent security arrangements unless we received a direct request of course.'

Mangini left the Vatican, aware that he was going to have a very unpleasant interview with his own superior officer. He wondered, not for the first time, if he should have joined his father in the wine trade. He might still do that.

Thursday, 8th February 1979.

The morning dawned cold and unfriendly. The sort of morning which gives notice to the sensitive that it is not going to be a good day.

Peter awoke suddenly at six o'clock after a restless sleep. He had been sitting with Spartov until the early hours. He was bleary with fatigue. His forehead felt as if the skin was made of elastic, a little too tight for his skull.

He had just finished washing and was carefully easing himself into his soutane (why did his shoulders ache so much?) when the knock sounded on his door. He was never to forget that knock. Three hard raps, urgent, demanding attention.

The Pope had suffered a sudden relapse and he was sinking fast. Peter hurried down unending corridors to the papal apartments.

When he got there, the room was a bustle of activity. The pope was already dead. Cardinal Bangio had just finished the age-old ritual of tapping his head three times with a silver hammer and calling the Pope by his own name – Wenceslas Tadeo Celavsky. He was about to remove the signet ring which Leo had only recently replaced on his finger. Two nuns were getting ready to prepare the body for traditional embalming, Carelli and a number of white- haired prelates were bowed in prayer at the foot of the bed. Professor Formenti had been and gone again, after certifying death by more orthodox methods, to collect the impedimenta of the embalmer. Outside the door, two Swiss guards stood stiffly at attention, four more stood at the corners of the bed. Peter performed the only service he could do for his old master and dropped to his knees in prayer.

Friday, 9th February 1979.

The news of the pope's death after less than a year on the throne of St Peter pushed all other news off the front page. The investigation into the carnage in Trastevere was reported in small type in most Italian newspapers and not at all on radio or TV. A police inspector was reported to believe that the victims were terrorists who had quarrelled and finally fallen victim to their own devices which had exploded prematurely. The revolving number plates had either been overlooked or the information was being suppressed.

***

Ambassador Puvinski was somewhat relieved by the Pope's sudden death, which was simply reported as due to 'sudden and severe internal bleeding,' because he had no idea how he would have arranged for a suitable accident as required by Moscow. He decided to say nothing, however, because he learned, by telephone, that he was to be decorated for special services to the Soviet Union. Even he saw the irony of it.

In accordance with longstanding papal custom, the Pope's body had not been subject to an autopsy but Professor Formenti remarked to Peter that he was puzzled about the small scars he had noticed in amongst the hairs and behind the ears of the dead pontiff.

'I usually only find scars like that in my patients who have had facelifts. Dr Uglev certainly records no facial surgery in his notes. Very curious.'

Peter took the first available opportunity, while mourning was in progress, to speak to Carelli about his many doubts about the Pope's sanity, his odd withdrawn behaviour at times and the facial scars. He saw the look in Carelli's eyes as they sat together in the Cardinal's study. It suggested that he was also concerned.

'You raise many interesting points' said Carelli, 'I will need some time to consider them and take some advice before taking any action.' Peter thanked him and left. Would he be retained as private secretary to whoever was elected at the forthcoming conclave? Whatever transpired Peter had an inkling that Vatican life still had much to offer.

EPILOGUE

Saturday, 3rd March 1979.

Russian spy Andrei Spartov had received a lying-in state in St Peter's Basilica, a pontifical funeral in St Peter's Piazza and had been buried in the grave of Leo XIV under St Peter's Basilica. The conclave area of the Vatican was almost ready for a new election.

Russian spy Leonid Nikitin aka Giorgio Carelli sat in his office and made a call using his burner phone. He was quickly connected. 'Listen Rostock. It is fortunate that you did not advise Spartov of my identity but a great pity that you did not warn me of his placement. It is going to take all my skill to unravel the effects of the Synod. In addition, Spartov had a private secretary called Peter Dunne. He is starting to ferret around and ask awkward questions. Get someone to remove him. Make it look like an accident or heart attack....'

ACKNOWLEDGEMENTS

My Daughter, the late Caroline Dalziel, read my rough draft. She made many helpful corrections and added many better and elegant words.

Lisa and Edward Douglas spent many hours helping me with useful advice and taking the book through the publication process. Without them the story would have remained on my computer.

Cover Design: L R Douglas and E Douglas

Printed in Great Britain
by Amazon